Lesley

THE COBWEB CLUB

THE COBWEB CLUB

by

DENNIS W. BOREHAM

VICTORY PRESS
EASTBOURNE

ISBN 0 85476 273 6

To the Lansdowne children

Printed in Great Britain for Kingsway Publications Limited, Lottbridge Drove, Eastbourne, E. Sussex BN23 6NT by Richard Clay (The Chaucer Press) Ltd., Bungay, Suffolk

CONTENTS

CHAPTER ONE

THE TIN CAN

'When will this rain go away?'

Tony was not in the habit of talking to himself, at least, not aloud. The summer holidays were already one week old and, ever since he had closed his desk at school with a joyful bang, the rain had hardly stopped at all.

'It wouldn't seem so bad if it was interesting rain,' he continued. 'Like they have at sea. But this dull drizzle!'

He peered across from where he stood on the fourth floor balcony of the block of flats in which he lived. The houses on the opposite hill, two miles away, were shrouded in a murky gloom, like an old grey blanket. It was only half past eight in the evening at the height of summer. He felt a flicker of comfort. The weather was the same for everybody, even for them! They lived in a different world; a world of lush green lawns carefully cut once a week by electric mowers; a world of landscaped gardens; a world of patios and double garages. He lived in The Flats.

Away to the north, at about five miles distance, the tall, slim buildings of Central London soared into the sky like huge mouth organs stood up on end waiting for a giant to come and wrap his lips around them and play a tune. The weather hid them from Tony's view.

Normally, at this time of evening, perhaps a little later, he would watch the concrete buildings come alive with light. He took his own mouth organ from his pocket and ran his lips up the scale. Then he stood it up on the balcony with the mouthpiece towards him, a miniature, metal, block of flats, unlit and cold.

Huge puddles made the tarmac below quite attractive when the wind blew them into little ripples. Once or twice a flat dweller scurried across from one block to another on some errand or visit. A man, who had been working late, trudged through the rain on his way home. The playground was deserted. The swings dripped water. The roundabout was still. He thought of all the children who would have been using the playground if the weather had been kind.

'They are all watching the telly, I suppose,' he murmured.

He was fed up with television. When there was a programme he wanted to see he couldn't watch it. Somebody else in the family always wanted to view the other channels.

'Your programmes are in the early part of the evening,' his father often said.

Tony sighed and screwed his fingers into the palms of his hands. Not one of his family seemed to realise that he was nearly twelve!

He decided to brave the weather and make a final circuit of The Flats before going indoors. Picking up his mouth organ, he ran down the stone steps at the end of the block, shunning the metal lift which was smelly, slow and unreliable. He kept close to the side wall where it was fairly dry and then leapt across the puddles to the next block. Nobody else was around.

At the back of The Flats the railway cut through a grassy embankment. A few cars were parked by the side of the high wire mesh fence. Just past the cars there was a huge, deep puddle, by far the biggest on the estate. Right in the middle of it sat a small tin can.

Tony grinned.

'I think I could kick that right over the fence,' he said.

And, without further thought, he raced through the water, not minding about his flimsy shoes or that his socks would be wringing wet.

Splash, splash, splash, splash! Kick! The tin can flew away in a stream of spray, hit the fence at high speed and skidded off behind a shed that was used as a store and was the property of the Council who owned The Flats.

Smash!

Tony's moment of happiness suddenly vanished. He had heard the sound of breaking glass too often to mistake it.

'Oh, no!' he cried. 'I haven't!'

But he had.

He eased his body between the boundary wire and the store. Glass was scattered everywhere. It had been quite a large window. He looked through the hole. It was nearly dark inside and difficult to see clearly. He slid out and looked around. Nobody had seen him. Nobody seemed even to have heard. He smiled to himself. For the first time that week he had something to look forward to. Tomorrow he wouldn't mind if it rained all day. Tomorrow he would investigate. Tomorrow he would climb into the shed.

CHAPTER TWO

TONY EXPLORES

When Tony awoke next morning a gap in the curtains let in the sun which shone straight on the picture of his favourite footballer stuck on the opposite wall. He swung out of bed and snatched the curtains aside. The sky was a very pale blue as though a young child had painted it by using too much water on the brush. But, at last, the rain had stopped. Already, a few early risers were in the playground. He could hear the squeaking of the swings.

'One of these days I'll take my oil can and fix those swings myself,' his father often said. But he had never done so.

After breakfast, Tony was free for the rest of the day, apart from putting in an appearance for meals. He sauntered out into the sunlight to see what was happening on the estate.

'Hiya, Tone,' a friend called.

'Hiya.'

'Come on the swings.'

Tony shook his head.

'No thanks. Not now. I might later.'

He turned the corner of his block. Several girls were playing with marbles near the wall. Tony stepped on one of the little glass balls accidentally and nearly fell over.

'Hey! Mind out! Clumsy!' a little girl cried. 'You're spoiling our game.'

'Sorry. I didn't tread on it on purpose,' Tony protested. 'How was I to know it was there?'

'Use your eyes then.'

This was the language of The Flats.

He ignored them and walked off towards the railway. The remains of the big puddle were still on the ground. He wondered what he would be doing if he hadn't seen the old tin can that had been sitting in the middle of it, waiting to be kicked. When he reached the shed and was ready to slip behind it out of sight a lady came out of a back entrance and he was in full view.

'Morning, Tony.'

He forced a smile.

'Hello, Mrs Morgan. Lovely day.'

Mrs Morgan hurried off without another word, clutching her shopping basket, intent on reaching the supermarket before it became crowded.

Tony thought how all adults seemed to be in a hurry; a continual race. He had time to spare. He carried on strolling. It mattered not that he had failed to enter the shed at the first attempt. He couldn't risk allowing anybody to see where he was going. It was his secret and he wasn't going to share it, no, not even with his friends.

On the next circuit of The Flats he was more fortunate. True, he met a number of children who wanted him to stop and talk, or to play games, but he made an excuse to be off. When he reached the shed, he pretended that his shoe lace was undone, bent down, looked around and then shot through the gap, by the fence, like an arrow. Now he could take his time.

He examined the window carefully. There wasn't very much left of it. He started to remove some of the jagged pieces of glass from the frame so that he could climb in without cutting himself. A train went by. He looked anxiously over his shoulder. He had quite forgotten about the trains. He would be in full view of the passengers on their way to London. But nobody seemed to notice. Indeed, if they had, they couldn't have done anything. He was the right side of the fence. He relaxed and made a good job of picking out the glass fragments. When he had finished, he climbed inside.

It was still quite gloomy inside, for the other, unbroken, windows were thick with dirt. Cobwebs hung everywhere. He wished he had brought a torch but then remembered that the batteries in his own torch were nearly finished and the feeble gleam wouldn't have been of much help to him. Besides, batteries were expensive. He looked around. The building was about fifteen metres long and five metres wide. The roof was about six metres high in the middle, pointed and sloping steeply to the sides like a capital V upside down.

'Plenty of space for games when the weather is bad,' he said, thoughtfully.

At one end, planks, trestles and step ladders were stacked against the wall. He walked across and felt the weight of one of the planks. It was heavy; and dirty too. He clapped his hands together and wiped them on his jeans. Near the door were some tins of paint, not the size he had seen in the shops but more like drums. He kicked one of them and then wished he hadn't.

'Ouch!'

It hurt.

All at once, he had the feeling that someone was watching him. Slowly, he glanced over his shoulder back to the window. Did somebody move? He couldn't be sure. He had felt uneasy ever since climbing into the shed. He knew he had no right to be there. He was a trespasser.

He turned round again and faced the paint drums, waiting for a full minute. Then, quickly, he swung on his heels, his sharp eyes ready. Nobody was there.

Suddenly, somebody sneezed! His muscles tightened and then, slowly, relaxed, one by one. It wasn't a man-sized sneeze.

'Where are you?' he called, softly, peering into the corners. 'Come on out. I won't hurt you.'

Gradually, a large tarpaulin began to move, like an old, brown animal waking up after a long sleep. A small cloud of dust floated up towards the roof, seeming to hang in the air on its way. Tony watched. Everything was happening in slow motion. Presently, a grubby little girl crawled out and stood up. She looked very guilty.

'Julie!' he exclaimed. 'What are you doing in here?'

Julie sniffed and rubbed her hands across her eyes.

'I was frightened when I heard somebody at the window,' she explained. 'I didn't know who it was. So I hid.'

Tony looked at her, kindly. How could he be cross with her? She was so much smaller than himself. She had as little right to be there as he had.

'There's no need to be afraid now. It's only me.'

Julie walked over to the window. In the better light Tony saw that her blue dress was torn near the hem.

'I suppose you tore that on the window. What will they say when you go home?'

Julie bent down and examined it.

'It's not much. I'm always tearing my dress on something or other. They are used to me at home.'

Tony smiled. That was true enough. Julie had often fallen off walls, out of trees, down stairs, off roundabouts and swings, even off a seesaw, tearing her clothes and bruising her body as though she had nine lives.

'You were lucky you didn't cut yourself, climbing in like that,' Tony scolded.

How had she managed not to!

Julie's eyes sparkled.

'It's easy when you know how,' she boasted. 'I've already broken my arm twice and my leg once. And I'm only nine. A little window like that wasn't hard.'

Tony grunted.

'Falling off walls isn't very clever,' he said.

Julie shrugged her shoulders and flung back her long hair.

'Well, it was clever to climb through without cutting myself on the broken glass,' she replied. 'Even if I did tear my dress!'

'Why did you climb in?' asked Tony. 'If you were frightened of the dark you should have stayed outside in the sunshine.'

'I didn't mean to climb in really,' she said. 'I didn't know I would be able to. I only saw the broken window when I walked behind the shed to pick those flowers by the wire.'

Tony looked at her hands.

'I see you found some,' he said. 'Julie! You are in a terrible mess!'

She wiped her hands down her dress.

'You don't look so smart yourself,' she replied.

Tony laughed.

'I'm not wearing my best clothes,' he said. 'But, now we have found a way into the shed, what are we going to do about it?'

He couldn't hope to keep it a secret now Julie had found a way in. The whole estate would know about it before dinner. All the children would want to see inside.

'It's nice and big,' Julie said, wistfully. 'And dirty! Look at all those cobwebs hanging from the roof!'

Tony looked up. His eyes had become used to the poor light.

'Like dusty curtains,' he said.

'I know! Let's clean it!' Julie exclaimed. 'Let's make it nice so we can play in here when it is raining outside.'

'Should we?'

Tony was fed up with the rain, too.

'Yes! Let's ...'

'Hey! Wait a minute!' Tony warned. 'It isn't our shed. Don't forget that.'

'It's on our estate,' Julie protested. 'Nobody else is using it. Why shouldn't we?'

Tony thought deeply. She was wrong, of course. Quite wrong. But, why shouldn't they use it? It was standing empty, or nearly empty. If they cleaned it and made it nice again, surely nobody would complain.

'All right,' he said, suddenly. 'All right. We can stick a notice on the board about it. The others are sure to help us.'

'A great big notice,' Julie said, spreading her thin arms as wide as they would go and making herself look like a miniature scarecrow. 'I have some crayons at home. What shall we call the shed? We must think of a good name.'

Tony looked up to the roof.

'The Cobweb Club!' he exclaimed.

Julie clapped her hands.

'I like that name,' she cried. 'Sounds good. We can do all sorts of interesting things. I'll put the notice up right away.'

Tony helped her over the window sill. Together, they slid back into the sunshine. The sky seemed to be a deeper blue.

'Looks much better now,' he said. 'I'll find some paper while you collect your crayons,' he suggested. 'Better have a wash, too. Meet at the playground in ten minutes.'

Julie was already skipping away.

The playground was the centre of activity for the younger boys and girls. If they wanted to meet it was always there, at the playground. It was shunned by the older ones, except, perhaps, when the young children were indoors and asleep. Then, the older ones would sit on the swings in the twilight, swapping jokes, laughing loudly and eating hot chips from a greasy bag. Here, too, another band of youths might come and wreck the swings so that the council had to repair them. When Tony arrived with a large piece of wallpaper, Julie was already instructing the other boys and girls.

'You've all got to help us,' she was saying. 'It's a big shed, it's ever so dirty and it will take a lot of hard work to clean it.'

'What are we going to do with it when it is clean?' one boy said. 'It isn't much fun working hard if we can't use the place.'

Julie turned to Tony for help.

'You tell them,' she pleaded.

The others gathered round Tony, who had always been the natural leader of this age group. He was the eldest and he often settled their arguments and saw that nobody was bullied. He had a reputation for being fair. They became very attentive.

'I haven't thought it out properly,' he admitted. 'But I am sure we can all have a lot of fun in the shed once we have cleaned it. We wouldn't have to stay indoors when it rains. It's a perfect place for all sorts of games.'

The children nodded in agreement. What Tony said made sense. Everybody had been fed up with the rain.

'What's the wallpaper for?' one of them asked.

'I thought we could make a notice and stick it on the wall at the end of The Flats. You know where I mean. There is a proper notice board.'

'Nobody ever looks at that,' somebody said. 'Anyway, we don't want a notice. We can tell all our friends.'

Tony rolled the paper tightly and stuck it under

his arm. He wasn't going to need it. Julie closed her pencil box with a bang.

'All right,' he said, making a sudden decision. 'Meet here after dinner at two o'clock. Bring all the brooms and buckets of water you can find.'

'And soap powder,' said Julie.

'And lots of cloths and old rags,' somebody else said.

'And dustpans!'

They were not short of ideas. The Cobweb Club was about to swing into action.

CHAPTER THREE

THE BIG CLEAN UP

Tony borrowed two old kitchen chairs from his mother. She didn't mind. Tony thought they would be useful in helping the children to climb over the window sill. Some of the children had quite small brothers and sisters who were sure to tag along just to see what was happening. He staggered down the stairs. The chairs were heavy. Most of the children were already waiting in the playground. When he saw them he smiled.

'You look like an army of cleaners,' he said, surveying his troops like a general.

They had piles of old rags, dusters, disinfectant, brooms and nearly everybody had a plastic bucket full of water.

'My mum doesn't know I've brought this,' one little girl said, proudly. 'She isn't in.'

Tony looked stern.

'Then take it back at once, before she comes home,' he said, firmly. 'We don't want to cause trouble. We'll wait for you. Hurry!'

The little girl took her broom back without one word of protest. Tony was in control.

'Right,' he continued. 'When she returns we walk round to the shed. It doesn't matter who sees us. We are going to do a job of work and nobody should mind that. Only, we'll do it properly. No messing about!'

When the little girl returned they marched off, about twenty in all, to the back of the estate. A few grown-ups paused from whatever they were doing to give the children amused glances. This new found energy and keenness to work hard couldn't last long. Adults always knew best!

The chairs were useful and the younger children scrambled easily over the window sill, which was quite a high one. Once inside, they sniffed around each corner and expressed their approval.

'It's great!'

'Marvellous!'

'A place of our own!'

'It is rather dirty, though,' one girl said. 'Where shall we begin?'

'Let's clean the good window,' Tony suggested. 'We shall be able to see better then.'

He carried the chairs to the other window and gave some of the girls a bucket of water and some rags. The others helped Tony clear some rubbish from around the door. To his delight somebody discovered a light switch.

'That won't work,' they all said.

But they were wrong. It did!

'That's the best discovery of the afternoon,' Tony said.

'And we've only been in here twenty minutes,' Julie said. 'Now we can really get to work.'

It was great fun. They dragged the step ladders across the floor, making sure that the ladders were as wide apart as possible. Carefully, and with great difficulty, they lifted the heavy planks.

'Just a little bit higher,' Tony said, as they man-handled the beams. 'Keep pushing!'

It took a long time and they had a rest before trying again but, in the end, they succeeded in making a cat-walk of planks beneath the roof. Soon, the children were running along them as though they had been labourers all their lives.

Tony looked anxious.

'Do be careful!' he shouted. 'We don't want any accidents.'

Julie sat on a plank above his head and grinned.

'Don't you worry about us, Tony. We are used to this.'

'We aren't all little monkeys like you, Julie,' he replied.

But he needn't have worried. The children seemed completely at home off the ground, just as he was of course, though he was much older and would take more care. There weren't any accidents, unless a bucket of water tipped over an unsuspecting boy from a great height was an accident. Unless another tear in Julie's dress was an accident. Unless a few splinters in several hands, unless ...

'We can't expect not to hurt ourselves sometimes, I suppose,' Tony said. 'Anybody good at getting splinters out?'

'We need a first aid box in here,' somebody suggested, sensibly.

'Now that is a good idea,' Julie replied. 'We can patch ourselves up before we go home. Might save a lot of angry words.'

At the end of two hours, when bucket after bucket of water had been used and more fetched from The

Flats, when the roof had been brushed with the special, long handled broom somebody had brought, when the good window was so clean you could watch the trains going by from inside the shed, when the rubbish had been piled outside, they decided they had done enough for one afternoon.

'Phew!'

They were all hot, tired and very dirty.

'Phew! Anybody got some lemonade?'

Tony stood back and looked at all they had done. Even he was pleased.

'It's a great start,' he said. 'Anybody coming back to do some more tomorrow?'

'Yes!'

They all promised to come.

'Good!'

Tony had formed a team, an unlikely team of children who normally might have been scrapping and quarrelling, but today had worked as one. He had become a leader. All because he had kicked an old tin can.

The next day the weather was fine and, despite the promises, not so many volunteers appeared.

'I've got to go shopping with my mum.'

'I promised to meet a friend.'

'My dad has the day off and I'm going out.'

'I want to watch the telly.'

Tony nodded, silently agreeing with all their reasons. He had expected this to happen. It wasn't quite so much fun to keep on doing something after the first time. Besides, not one of them knew if they would be able to use the shed or what they would put in it when they had finished cleaning it. It wasn't a lot of use empty, except, perhaps, for ball games.

'What would you really like to do in here?' he asked his dozen helpers when they were halfway through the afternoon.

'Pets,' a boy said. 'We aren't allowed to keep them indoors, but we could have some in here.'

'Oh yes!' Julie exclaimed. 'We could have rabbits and guinea pigs and mice and budgies and ...'

'Budgies don't like the dark very much,' somebody interrupted.

'It is a lot lighter now we have cleaned the window,' Julie protested. 'Anyway, we could leave the light on sometimes.'

'And could we pay the bill?' Tony asked.

They hadn't thought of that.

'Electricity isn't cheap,' he said.

'What we need is some money,' Julie said, suddenly. 'We could do all sorts of things if we had some money, you know, nice things like making barrows. We don't always want to play, do we? I get fed up with playing.'

'That sounds all right,' someone said. 'I like making models but I was told off at home when I spilled some glue over the carpet.'

Tony laughed.

'There's no carpet in here,' he said, kicking the floor. 'You won't get told off here.'

'We could have the pets in one corner,' suggested Julie. 'There is plenty of room.'

'All right. We can. First, though, we must make the hutches for the animals to use. For that we need wood. And wood is expensive.'

'Like electricity,' somebody said.

'So we must have some money,' Julie said.

'How?'

Tony was making them think. They knew it wasn't easy to earn money. They were all far too young to work and they weren't very good at saving what was given them by aunts and uncles. The sweet shop was near The Flats. It was hard to walk by.

'I know!'

One of the boys had an idea.

'Let's go around the streets and clean some cars. There are lots and lots of cars. Most of them could do with a good clean.'

'Great!'

They were all excited about the idea.

'Great! How much shall we charge?'

'Hey! Wait a minute,' Tony said. 'If we do this then it must be on a proper basis.'

'Listen to him,' Julie laughed. 'A proper basis! He's been watching too much telly.'

'Shut up,' Tony said, rudely. 'If we clean cars we'll clean them properly and not charge too much. And we'll not stick out our tongues at people who don't want us to clean their cars. Or slam their gates. Understand?'

'Yes, sir,' Julie mocked. 'Oh, stop it, Tony. You sound just like Mr Jenkins at school.'

'Well, we must do things properly,' he insisted. 'It's a very good idea. Let's not charge anything.'

'What?'

'Do it for nothing?'

'No fear!'

They were not prepared to do that.

'No,' Tony explained. 'We can take whatever people

think it's worth. That will help us to do a good job.'

They all nodded their agreement.

'That isn't a bad idea, I suppose,' somebody said.

'I shall be cross if I clean some cars and then the people are out when I knock at their doors or, worse still, won't answer.'

Tony tried to be patient.

'You knock first, ask politely, if they want to know how much you charge tell them they can give you what they like when you have finished the job,' he explained.

'And ask them for some clean water to put in your bucket,' Julie said.

She had the right idea.

'I don't think I want to do it on my own,' a girl said. 'It would be much better if we went in twos or threes. More fun.'

Tony thought for a moment. He wasn't too sure.

'What do you think?' he asked.

'In pairs,' Julie said. 'And I'll come with you!'

Tony shrugged his shoulders.

'If you like,' he said. 'I don't mind. So long as you do your share.'

So it was settled.

When Tony went indoors he told his parents all about the shed and their plans for raising money by cleaning cars.

'It sounds all right to me,' his father said. 'At least you will be doing something useful with your time.'

'It's a pity the council doesn't do more for the kids around this estate,' his mother said, putting her hands on her hips as she always did when she had something important to say or she was cross. 'I don't think they

even considered the children when they built The
Flats. Can't do this! Can't do that! Mustn't walk on
the grass!'

'Grass! Most of that disappeared after the first week,'
his father scoffed. 'They needn't have bothered to lay
the turfs. Couple of dozen kids with a football soon
kicked that lot up. And broke the notice about not
walking on it!'

'Well, what do you expect?' his mother replied.
'The kids need somewhere to play.'

'That is why we want to use the big shed,' Tony
explained. 'I hope the council won't stop us.'

His father folded his newspaper and wagged his
finger.

'I'll tell you something,' he began. 'If they do stop
them they will have me to contend with.'

He drew himself up to his full height and flexed
his muscles.

'The kids deserve somewhere to themselves. So long
as they don't make trouble.'

So Tony had his parents on his side. He was
pleased. It wasn't very often that an idea of his own
met with such instant approval. He hoped the grown-
ups in the council offices would be as understanding.
They were sure to find out what was happening sooner
or later.

Next morning, when Tony made his way to the
kitchen for his breakfast, he discovered that his father,
who had already left for work, had found a leather
and some good, soft cloth for him to use.

'And you can take the red plastic bucket,' his mother
said. 'It's not over big.'

'Thanks.'

Tony tucked into his breakfast.

'I think Julie is going to bring another bucket, he said, between mouthfuls. 'And some yellow dusters.'

His mother nodded.

'Very well,' she said. 'Then you will have everything you need. Keep your eye on young Julie. She always seems to be getting into mischief.'

Tony laughed.

'I know,' he replied. 'But she asked to come with me and she really has worked very hard in the shed.'

His mother looked doubtful.

'It probably won't last,' she warned. 'Watch her. She's like a little monkey sometimes.'

'Yes, Mum.'

Tony thought his mother was being a little unfair.

'I'll be home for dinner,' he said.

His mother laughed.

'I've not known you miss your dinner yet,' she said.

Julie was waiting in the playground when he went downstairs.

'Some of the others have gone already,' she said.

She wanted to be first and sounded annoyed.

'I had to eat my breakfast,' Tony replied. 'Have you had yours?'

'Yes. Not so much as you though, I don't expect.'

'Which way did the others go?' he asked.

'Most of them went up the hill.'

Tony nodded.

'That's the best part,' he said. 'All those nice little houses without garages. The cars are nose to tail in the street.'

'Like a long, tin caterpillar,' Julie said. 'Getting dirtier and dirtier every day.'

She picked up her bucket.

'Come on, Tony,' she said, pulling his arm. 'We don't want the others to take all the best jobs before we arrive.'

They started off up the hill.

'I think we shall find somebody who wants their car cleaned,' Julie said, swinging her bucket.

'I hope you are right.'

They turned a corner and saw two girls from The Flats hard at work.

'Hello!'

The girls were happily polishing a big, white car.

'Hello!'

'Was it very dirty when you started?' Julie asked.

'Shoosh! Not so loud. The people might hear.'

'Was it?' Julie whispered.

'Terrible! But, look at it now!'

'It looks good to me,' Tony said.

'The lady next door came out just now, had a careful look and then told us we could clean her car after we have finished this one.'

Julie looked quite envious.

'Come along then, Julie,' Tony said. 'Let's walk along the next road and start knocking on the doors.'

They said goodbye to the workers and hurried off. It wasn't going to be very easy to knock on somebody's door and not run away.

'You can have the first knock,' Tony offered when they reached the right road. 'Ladies first!'

Julie looked shy; a most unusual look for her.

'No, thank you. You are the eldest. But I'll be right beside you. Don't worry!'

Tony sighed.

'All right. Then you can take the next one. That's fair.'

They opened a gate and closed it behind them with care. Tony smoothed his hair, dusted his jeans and looked at the bells.

'No use just looking at them,' Julie whispered.

'Which one shall I ring?' he asked.

'Ring them all,' she suggested. 'There are three cars outside. We might get three jobs at one go.'

'That's being greedy,' he said.

He rang. They waited. Nothing happened.

'Let me have a go!' she exclaimed, losing her patience.

She pushed Tony aside and, before he could stop her, she rang all the other bells.

'There!' she said. 'That should wake somebody. They can't all be out.'

She was right.

CHAPTER FOUR

TWO NEW FRIENDS

'Julie! You shouldn't have done that!'

Tony was very annoyed.

There was swift movement from inside the house. Somebody was coming. Quickly!

'There's still time,' Julie said, nervously. 'Come on, Tony. Let's run away.'

He caught her by the shoulder just as she reached the gate and steered her back to the doorstep.

'It isn't any use running away,' he said. 'That will make the people angrier still. We've got to face the music now.'

The door was flung open and a very angry woman glared down at them. Tony caught a glimpse of another woman, a smaller one, making her way along the passage. A foreign looking gentleman was halfway down the stairs.

'Did you ring all those bells?' the woman demanded.

Tony stepped back a full pace. The woman had enormous forearms and a floor-brush in her hand. She looked as if she might use it on him.

'I didn't ring the bells,' Tony replied. 'I am sorry you were alarmed. My friend was excited and she rang them all before I could stop her.'

The woman looked at Julie who was taking cover

behind Tony.

'Don't hide,' she bawled. 'You are old enough to know better. I was just about to get my cakes out of the oven.'

She departed, still waving her brush in the air.

'What is the matter?' the other woman asked. 'What are you doing on my doorstep?'

She was obviously the owner of the house. She eyed the buckets.

'What are you? A cleaning up brigade?'

Her voice sounded very unkind.

'We wondered if you wanted your car cleaned,' Tony said.

'Humph! I haven't got a car and if I had one I should clean it myself. Anyway, you shouldn't come around the streets trying to get money. It's as bad as begging.'

'We are not begging!' Tony exclaimed. 'We are quite prepared to work hard.'

'But you want paying for it, I am sure! Then, I suppose, you will go and waste the money on sweets.'

She dismissed them with a wave of her hand and turned to go indoors. Tony and Julie turned away also, towards the gate.

'Excuse me, please. Don't go away. What exactly do you do?'

They turned to see the foreign gentleman smiling at them.

'Don't you have anything to do with them,' the owner of the house called over her shoulder as she retreated into the interior. 'They won't do the job properly. They only want your money!'

The foreign gentleman winced.

'I am so sorry,' he said, kindly. 'My landlady does not have a very high opinion of you. I suppose it was because of the bells. But you don't look too bad to me. What exactly do you do and why do you do it? I should like to help if I can.'

'We clean cars,' Julie said, finding her tongue at last. 'We clean cars very nicely.'

The foreign gentleman smiled.

'I am sure you do,' he continued. 'But, how many have you cleaned today? Your buckets and sponges look very dry.'

'Well, actually, we haven't cleaned any,' Tony admitted. 'This is the first house we have tried.'

The foreign gentleman laughed.

'Then you haven't made a very good start, have you?' he said.

Tony shook his head.

'No. We haven't.'

'And why do you want to do this job? Is it for a good cause?'

'Oh, yes, it is,' Tony said. 'The money is for the Cobweb Club.'

'The Cobweb Club? What is that?'

They explained all that they were trying to do and why they needed somewhere to call their own, where they would be happy and free.

The foreign gentleman looked sympathetic.

'I should not like to live in The Flats,' he said. 'It is bad enough living here.'

He dropped his voice to a whisper.

'It is terrible living here,' he continued. 'So noisy!'

Tony and Julie understood.

'You may clean my car and, if you do it nicely, I

shall pay you well. My car is the green one. This is my bell, the one marked A. Monsingh, the second one from the top. You will remember that, won't you?'

'We will,' Tony promised. 'Can you give us some water, please?'

Mr Monsingh took their buckets and went upstairs again.

'There!' Julie exclaimed, happily. 'I knew this would be our lucky day.'

'It very nearly wasn't,' Tony replied. 'That big lady almost hit me with her brush. She was very cross. You mustn't ever do anything like that again.'

Mr Monsingh returned with the water.

'There you are,' he said, handing them the buckets carefully. 'Let me know when you have finished, please.'

'Thanks.'

Both Tony and Julie were truly grateful. It was their very first job. They would do it well.

'Which part should we clean first?' Julie asked. 'The top?'

'Yes, I'll do that,' Tony said. 'You won't be able to reach it. If you just wait a minute while I do the roof, we can do the rest of the car together. You can clean the front, if you like. I'll clean the back and then we can wash the sides. We may need some more water before then.'

'The car is rather dirty,' Julie admitted. 'We can do the wheels last of all. Look at all the mud on them! We ought to have brought a little brush with us.'

The system worked well. In ten minutes the car looked better. In half an hour it gleamed and the sun shone on the mirrors. They were ready to clean the wheels.

'I'll ask for some more water,' Tony said.

'Perhaps he will lend you a brush,' Julie suggested. 'These wheels need more than a sponge to get them clean.'

Tony remembered which bell to press. Mr Monsingh came down after a little while.

'I am sorry to have kept you waiting,' he apologised. 'I was ironing a shirt. How are you getting on?'

'Very well, thank you. We need some clean water for the wheels. If you have a small brush we could borrow it would be a great help on the wheels.'

'Yes, the wheels are very dirty. I had to go down to the country yesterday. It was very muddy. The car was in an awful state. I'll get the water.'

Tony waited. He felt very pleased that they had met such an understanding customer.

'Thanks,' he said, when Mr Monsingh returned. 'We shall be finished in five minutes. Then you can inspect the car.'

'I think it looks mervellous,' Julie said, when they had completed the job. 'How much shall we ask? It was ever so dirty!'

'We won't ask for anything,' Tony said, firmly. 'Remember? We all agreed. We take what we are given.'

'Oh, all right.'

Julie was anxious to make a lot of money in a short time. She wanted to buy some pets.

They rang the bell again and the gentleman came to inspect their work. He walked around the car, thoughtfully, rubbing his chin with his hand.

'What do you think of it? Is it all right?' Julie asked.

He smiled at them.

'You can come and clean my car every Saturday if you like,' he said. 'It hasn't been so clean since I bought it.'

He pulled some coins from his pocket and then put them back again.

'I like your idea of the Cobweb Club,' he said. 'So, this time, I'll give you a pound note.'

Tony's eyes lit up and Julie jumped in the air three times and clapped her hands.

'Oh, thank you!' Tony exclaimed, as Mr Monsingh took the note from his wallet. 'Thank you very much!'

'I can't promise to give you so much next Saturday,' he replied. 'But this is the very first car you have cleaned. So it is rather special, isn't it? I wish you success in what you are trying to do.'

Tony handed back the brush, but Mr Monsingh wouldn't take it.

'It's a very old brush,' he said. 'And I have another one upstairs. You keep it. It will be useful for the other cars. They all have wheels, you know, though I hope they won't all be as muddy as mine.'

'Goodbye, then,' Tony said, putting the note away in his pocket. 'And thank you very much indeed.'

'Goodbye until next Saturday.'

They picked up their buckets and continued down the road.

'I feel as if I'm walking on air,' Julie cried.

'Me, too.'

Tony could hardly believe their good fortune. A pound note for cleaning just one car! A regular contract each week!

'You know, Julie,' he said, thoughtfully. 'I know

our little club is going to succeed.'

'Of course it is!' she exclaimed. 'Come on. Let's find another beautiful dirty car!'

But it wasn't very easy. Although they were very polite and careful not to annoy, nobody else in that road seemed to require their services.

'We like to clean it ourselves,' some residents said.

'Our own children clean the car and we pay them.'

'Sorry, love. We cleaned it yesterday.'

'Thank you very much. Sorry to have troubled you,' was Tony's usual reply.

Julie, at least, was having a valuable lesson in manners.

'I hope the others have had a better time,' she sighed, after they had knocked on twenty doors.

'Doesn't anybody else want their car cleaned?'

'Cheer up, Julie,' Tony said. 'We had a lovely surprise with our first car and we can come back next Saturday.'

Julie nodded.

'Yes. He was a nice man,' she said. 'Much better than all those ladies were. They were proper old crabs!'

'Shoosh! Not so loud!'

When they reached the last house in the road without any more success they hadn't the heart to continue.

'It's nearly dinner time,' Tony said, hoping his companion would take the hint and suggest returning to The Flats.

'Let's go home then. We can try again this afternoon. It will be fun to find out how the others managed. I bet they have all earned more money than us.'

Julie was feeling discouraged. She had expected everybody would want their car cleaned. She had found out that grown-ups didn't always do what children wanted.

When they reached The Flats some of their friends met them.

'How did you get on?' Tony asked. 'Did you have any luck?'

'Yes. We made eighty pence.'

'We made over a pound!'

'I only made thirty pence. I'm not trying any more, I don't think it's worth the bother.'

'What about the others?' Julie asked.

'Jean and Janet made over two pounds,' somebody said. 'Nobody turned them down.'

'Phew!' Tony replied. 'We made a pound and we hope to have another go this afternoon. Cheer up! At this rate, we won't have to go around working for very long.'

He tried to do some mental arithmetic. If they had some success after dinner, they might have enough money to buy some wood. It would be good to start making the hutches for the animals. That would be real progress!

'If you see any of the others,' he said. 'Tell them to meet at the shed at six o'clock this evening. We'll count the money then.'

He turned to Julie.

'See you at two?'

She nodded.

'Yes, I'll feel more like work after dinner.'

Tony went indoors and told his mother all about their morning.

'I told you to keep an eye on young Julie,' she said, when she heard about the bell ringing.

'I think she learned her lesson,' Tony said. 'The lady on the door step was very angry. Julie hid behind me. It's not like her to be frightened of anybody.'

'She probably thought the woman was going to clobber her with the brush,' his mother continued. 'Might have knocked some sense into her.'

'Oh, Julie isn't that bad,' Tony said. 'She worked jolly hard on the car. It looked really nice when we had finished it.'

'It was good of the man to let you clean it again next week. And a pound note! Well!'

'He was very kind,' Tony agreed. 'What have we got for dinner, Mum?'

'I suppose you're hungry enough to eat two dinners. You usually come in starving. Well, I bought some of those nice big sausages from the butcher. I know you like them better than the ones from the super-market. I had to queue for them, mind, so eat them all up.'

Tony smiled.

'You're joking,' he said. 'I promise to eat everything you give me.'

And he did.

Julie was waiting at the foot of the stairs when Tony went down at two o'clock.

'Feel better now?' he asked.

'Yes,' she said, 'I had sausages for dinner.'

'So did I.'

They walked through The Flats and across the street. An ice cream van waited by the side of the road. Julie looked at Tony.

'All right,' he said, reading her thoughts. 'I'll pay. But with my own money. What we earn is strictly for the club.'

Julie's face split into a huge smile.

'You're great, Tony,' she said. 'I'll work ever so hard this afternoon.'

They collected their ice creams and wandered slowly up the hill. The sun shone down and the ice cream melted and ran up Julie's arm.

'I'm getting in an awful mess,' she said, licking her wrist. 'Why does the sun have to shine and melt the ice cream? I was trying to make mine last a long time.'

'I'm pleased to see the sun,' Tony said. 'If it was raining we wouldn't be able to clean any cars. It can rain as much as it likes tomorrow. We'll be in the shed making hutches.'

'My mum would call that selfish,' Julie said.

And Tony had to agree, silently, that it was.

They made their way through the area they had worked that morning to another street.

'No garages,' Julie said, happily. 'And lots of cars.'

They knocked at a door. Nothing happened.

'Shall I knock again?' Julie asked.

'Yes. Just once more. They might not have heard the first time.'

They knocked and waited. Suddenly, somebody started to come downstairs. They gripped their buckets and waited.

'Can we clean your car for you, please?' Tony asked, when she had opened the door.

The lady smiled.

'Depends on how much you charge,' she replied.

'As much as you like,' Julie said, quickly.

'Or as little,' added Tony.

'You mean I can pay you whatever I think the job is worth?'

'Yes.'

The lady looked thoughtful.

'Why are you doing all this work?' she asked.

So they explained about the Cobweb Club.

'Sounds like a good idea,' the lady said, after she had listened patiently, without interrupting. 'Very well. I'll get some water, or, better still, you can come up and get it yourself. Would you like a drink and a piece of cake before you start?'

Tony was about to explain that they had just had their dinner and an ice cream, but Julie was too quick for him.

'Ooh, yes please, miss!' she said, eagerly.

The lady smiled again.

'Follow me upstairs to the kitchen then,' she said.

Julie nudged Tony. This really was their lucky day and no mistake!

The kitchen was small but tidy. A row of copper saucepans hung on the wall.

'Ooh, I like those,' Julie said.

'Do you? What do you like about them?'

Julie thought hard.

'I'm not sure,' she said. 'Perhaps it's because they look so shiny and warm.'

The lady turned to Tony.

'The cake tin is on the shelf above the saucepans. I put it up high so I can't reach it too easily.' she said. 'Would you get it for me, please?'

Tony did as he was asked and put the tin on the table.

'Here's a knife,' the lady said, offering it to Julie. 'You can cut the cake today.'

Julie's face glowed with happiness. She had never been allowed to cut a big cake before.

'Shall I cut you the first slice, miss?' she asked. 'Just a small slice?'

The lady laughed.

'Why not?' she said. 'I haven't had my lunch yet. I have been out shopping. If you had called ten minutes earlier you wouldn't have found me in.'

Tony thought how glad he was that she had answered the door. There was something very different about her. He couldn't decide what it was. Something specially nice, though.

'There you are, miss,' Julie said, offering the small slice to the lady.

'Thank you very much, Julie.'

She turned to Tony.

'And you are Tony,' she said. 'I heard you both outside the house.'

Tony smiled.

'I wondered how you knew,' he replied.

'My friends call me Shan.'

Tony wanted to say that Shan was a funny name for such a nice lady, but he didn't. He felt so surprised that she wanted them to be her friends.

'Shan,' he said, munching his piece of cake and holding his glass of orange squash. 'Shan. Yes, I like that very much.'

Shan laughed.

'I'm glad you approve,' she said.

When they had finished their refreshments they filled their buckets at the sink and went downstairs.

Shan showed them the car.

'It's the little green one,' she explained.

'We like cleaning green cars best of all,' Julie said, happily.

But she didn't say why.

CHAPTER FIVE

TONY WRITES A LETTER

'I think Shan is super!' Julie said after Shan had gone indoors. 'The way she let me cut that cake! My mum would have had the horrors!'

Tony agreed. He was busy surveying the car.

'Let's do it real special,' he said. 'Even if it takes us all the afternoon.'

They washed the car carefully, fetched some clean water from Shan's kitchen and washed it again. Tony brushed the wheels while Julie polished the chrome. They had just finished when somebody walked by.

'Who asked you to clean it?' a lady asked. 'This is a surprise!'

'We knocked at the door,' Tony explained.

'Which door?'

Julie pointed.

'The green one,' she said. 'Shan lives there.'

'Oh, Shan! But this isn't her car. She hasn't got a car.'

Slowly, Tony realised what had happened.

'It's your car, isn't it?' he said. 'Shan knew you wanted it cleaned.'

'The car belongs to my husband. He has been in bed for a fortnight. His back is bad. I expect Shan wanted to do us a good deed. She is like that.'

Tony nodded.

'Sounds like Shan,' he said.

'Well, do you think we have cleaned it nicely?' Julie asked.

The lady stood back a pace or two.

'It looks marvellous!' she said. 'And I shall reward you for your hard work, of course. Wait a moment while I take my shopping indoors, please.'

She took out her key and hurried down her garden path. When she was safely inside her house and out of earshot, Tony spoke to Julie.

'We can't take her money. It wouldn't be fair.'

Julie didn't like the thought of having worked so hard for nothing.

'I suppose it would spoil things for Shan,' she admitted. 'But what about the club? What will the others say when we tell them we cleaned somebody's car for nothing. They will think we are daft! I do wish the lady hadn't come back from shopping just now. Shan would have paid us well.'

'Come on, anyway,' Tony said. 'Let's go now.'

They picked up their buckets and hurried down the street and around the corner out of sight.

'I'm not sorry she came back,' Tony continued. 'It feels good to do something for nothing especially for the man who has hurt his back. He needed a bit of help.'

'And he got us,' Julie said, proudly.

After tea, the gang met in the shed. Their entrance didn't cause any stir among the people on the estate. It was common knowledge, by this time, that the children had taken over the store shed. Most of the others were there when Tony climbed through the window, book in hand, pencil stuck behind his left ear and a small bag slung over his shoulder.

'What's all the gear for?' a girl asked.

'The money,' Tony explained. 'And the book is to write all the amounts in.'

'Everything must be proper,' Julie said.

She believed in Tony now.

'Well? How much?' Tony asked, looking at the first pair.

'Two pounds thirty five pence,' they said, proudly. 'Here, count it carefully. It is all there.'

Tony dropped some of the coins and they scrambled after them on the concrete floor.

'Here. Give me the book,' Julie said. 'Tell me how much and I'll write it down for you. That way we'll be finished quicker. I've got to have a bath tonight.'

So they continued, growing more excited as the total mounted, until they discovered that they had earned over twelve pounds between them. It was beyond their wildest dreams.

'Let's go out again tomorrow,' somebody suggested.

Tony wasn't in favour.

'No,' he said. 'I vote we do something different tomorrow. Let's buy some wood and beg some boxes. We can start to make the hutches for our pets. Then, the next day, perhaps we can buy some guinea pigs.'

'Oh, yes!'

They were easily persuaded.

'We shall need tools,' he continued. 'A decent saw. Hammers. Nails. Screwdrivers. Screws.'

He tried to remember all the tools he had used in the workshop at school the previous term. He was quite good at woodwork and it would be great fun making the hutches without a teacher being near.

'I know a greengrocer who will let me have some boxes,' somebody said.

'I can bring some wire netting,' another offered.

'I can ...'

They were all eager to help.

'Good!' Tony said, holding up his hands. 'Bring anything that might be useful. We can buy what we have to. Meet here at ten o'clock.'

'Can't we meet earlier?'

'Half past nine then. But we need time to collect what we can.'

That evening, when most of the children had gone to bed, Tony sat on the steps at the side of his block playing his mouth organ. It had been a very successful day. The money was safely locked away in his bedroom. His mum and dad had listened in silence while he told them the full story of the day's events. More than ever, he was glad he had kicked the old tin can. As he sat there, letting his mouth run up the scale, he couldn't help thinking of Shan. What was it that made her different? She hadn't fussed over them like most grown-ups. She had left them to wash the car without so much as a peep around the curtains, as far as he knew. She had treated them as though they were like herself; as though she was like them; as though they were equal.

'Equal,' he said, out loud.

He played his fastest tune until he was out of breath and then sat quietly wiping his mouth organ on his handkerchief. His mother was always telling him not to do that. Unhygienic, she would say. Suddenly, he was aware of footsteps on the tarmac. It wasn't a man, the pace was too quick. He played another, slower, tune. Somehow, he knew who was coming to meet him. She found him by the wall.

'Hello, Tony.'

'Shan,' he said. 'I thought it was you.'

She sat down beside him on the steps. On the steps!

'There's a seat,' Tony said, pointing to the playground. 'It will be more comfortable.'

'This is all right for me if it's all right for you,' Shan replied.

She was wearing a trouser suit. It was dark blue. She had a flimsy scarf tied around her neck. Her hair was neat and light. It had just been washed.

'Gentlemen don't stare at ladies,' she said, laughing.

Tony felt embarrassed.

'I'm sorry,' he stammered. 'I just wondered why ...'

'Why I'm here?' she said, completing the sentence for him.

'Yes.'

'Well, you ran off before I could pay you, didn't you?'

Tony nodded.

'We couldn't take your money,' he said. 'It wasn't your car. The man couldn't clean it himself.'

'Mrs Bennett came back a little too early,' Shan said, kindly.

Tony thought about that and, for a minute or two, they sat in silence, side by side.

'I don't think she did,' Tony said, at last. 'It made us feel good to do something worthwhile to help somebody. The money spoils it, I suppose.'

Shan agreed.

'I know what you mean,' she said. 'But you were working for a good cause.'

She looked around the estate.

'There isn't much room for playing games here,' she continued.

'And only one seat on the whole estate for the old people,' Tony said.

Shan laughed.

'Then I am glad I didn't sit on it,' she said. 'I'm not old yet!'

'We collected over twelve pounds,' Tony said.

'Really!'

It was Shan's turn to be surprised.

'Really? What have you done with all the money?'

'It's all counted, written down in a book and locked away,' Tony said.

'Everything done properly,' Shan said.

'Yes.'

Tony sat up straight and stuffed his handkerchief in his pocket.

'Yes. Everything done properly,' he repeated.

Shan fell silent for a moment.

'What are you going to buy?' she asked, eventually.

'Wood for hutches, nails, screws. Anything we need. All tomorrow.'

'And the day after tomorrow?'

'Buy the animals, perhaps.'

Shan didn't reply and Tony was rather disappointed. He wanted her approval.

'Well?' he asked. 'What do you think?'

'Not bad,' she said. 'But ...'

'But, what?'

'But, what do the council think about all this?'

'They don't know,' Tony admitted. 'It worries me. I suppose they will throw us out when they know we are in their shed.'

'They may do,' Shan said.

'Then, what would we do with the animals?' Tony asked, half talking to himself. 'Where would we put them?'

Shan didn't answer and Tony realised that she was making him think for himself.

Suddenly, Shan stood up.

'Will you let me see your shed?' she asked.

'Oh, yes.'

Tony was pleased she wanted to see it.

'I'll take you to it now while there is still some light left. Otherwise, you won't see a thing.'

'You will have to squeeze by the wire,' Tony explained when they reached the shed.

But Shan wouldn't.

'No,' she said, firmly. 'I'll see the inside of your shed and all the things you have done when I can walk through the door. And not before then!'

'But the council!' Tony exclaimed. 'You will never be able to do what you say.'

'Never? Never is a long time,' Shan said, walking away. 'I think it will be soner than that.'

Tony hurried after her.

'How, Shan? How?'

She looked him straight in the eye, a strong, commanding look.

'That is for you to find the answer, Tony,' she said.

Long after, in the dark hours of the night, Tony lay on his bed, tossing and turning, unable to sleep. It was a hot, sticky night, but the reason for his sleeplessness wasn't the heat. It was his thoughts.

'That is for you to find the answer,' she had said,

as if she knew what to do but wouldn't tell him. He had to think things out for himself. At first he felt annoyed, even angry, but after a little while he began to realise how wise she was, and how different. She was on his side and he knew he could count on her for support. But, how? Eventually, when the new dawn was ready to scratch the sky with fiery fingers, he fell asleep. For once, his mother had to awaken him.

When the postman called while Tony was having his breakfast, the idea Shan wanted him to have came to him. Of course! A letter! He could write to the council and tell them what he was trying to do. He would own up about the window and ask permission to use the shed. They might even help!

He finished his toast and helped his mother dry the dishes.

'Where do I send a letter to the council, Mum?' he asked.

She turned to face him. A frown was on her face.

'The council!' she exclaimed. 'Whatever do you want to write to them for?'

'About the shed. I want permission to use it. I want them to open the door. I want to go in the proper way. I want people to see what we are trying to do. I want...'

'You want a lot, my boy,' she said. 'If I know anything about the council they will board up that window and you won't be able to get in any way, proper or otherwise. It won't be any good writing to the council.'

But she was wrong, and Tony knew in his heart that she was. He didn't say anything but decided to write the letter and to show it to Shan. She would know where to send it. After he had finished helping with the chores he found an old exercise book and a pen. He had the outline of a letter in his mind and he wanted to put his thoughts into words before he forgot.

'Dear Sir,' he began, but crossed it out.

'Your Worship.'

That sounded too grand, even for the mayor.

'Dear Mr Mayor.'

Yes. That was better, although he didn't know whether the present mayor was a man or a woman. He hadn't taken much notice of local affairs. Shan would know. He would ask her about that too.

'Dear Mr Mayor,

My name is Tony and I live on the estate up Lansdowne Hill, flat 25, Norwich House. A lot of children live on the estate and we don't have very much room to play. When it rains we have to stay indoors. There is an old store shed at the back of The Flats which belongs to the council. It is never used. Two nights ago, I broke a window by accident and then I climbed inside. I am sorry I broke the window. I didn't mean to. Some friends of mine have helped me clean out the shed and we want to use it ourselves. We have formed a club called The Cobweb Club. We are going to keep pets in the shed and make models and other interesting things.'

Tony read what he had written. He wasn't too happy about the window or too sure what the mayor would say about it. He thought it best to own up to it right away and hope that the mayor believed his story about it being an accident. The letter was already quite long, but he had to finish it properly.

'We shall be very grateful if you will arrange for a man to come and unlock the door so we can get in the proper way. Also, could the man mend the window and I will pay for it? It will be nice to have somewhere of our own and we promise to keep it tidy.'

That would do, he thought. Shan would know how to write the very last bit. He wasn't sure. Whenever he wrote to his aunt, which wasn't often, he always sent his love, but he didn't think the mayor would want that. He had just finished when the doorbell rang. Julie was at the door with ten other children.

'They can't come in. I've just scrubbed the floor,' Tony's mother shouted.

Tony trod carefully.

'I'll be back for dinner,' he called, as he went out.

'Mums!' Julie exclaimed, when they were out of earshot.

Julie had a healthy respect for Tony's mum.

'Nothing wrong with my mum,' Tony said, stoutly. 'Best cook in The Flats!'

CHAPTER SIX

THE ARRIVAL OF THE ANIMALS

'I thought we arranged to meet at the shed,' Tony protested, when they reached the foot of the stone stairs.

'You said half past nine, Tony,' one of the boys reminded him. 'It's nearly quarter past ten now.'

'We thought we would come to fetch you,' Julie explained. 'It's hard hanging around waiting when there are so many exciting things to do.'

Tony nodded.

'I'm sorry,' he apologised. 'I didn't mean to keep you all waiting but I've been trying to write a letter about the shed. It isn't any use carrying on like we do now, climbing through the window.'

'You mean climbing through where the window used to be,' somebody said.

'Oh, be serious,' Julie said to them all. 'Don't you see? If Tony has written a letter we might be turned out. Who did you write to?'

Tony hesitated. He didn't want them to laugh at him and he was beginning to wonder if he had acted wisely.

'Oh, nobody special,' he said, mysteriously. 'I haven't quite finished it, but I'll show it to you all in a few days. Then I shall post it.'

And they had to be content with that.

'Now,' he continued, surveying his troops. 'We mustn't all go down to the High Street shops in a gang this size. People might be knocked over.'

Julie laughed.

'Let's split up, then,' she suggested.

'Agreed?'

They all nodded.

'What have we brought?'

Tony didn't want to buy anything that wasn't necessary.

'I've brought some wire netting.'

'I've brought a hammer.'

'So have I, and two screwdrivers.'

'I've brought a saw.'

'I've brought an old box.'

Nearly everybody had managed to bring something.

'It's wood we need most of,' Tony said, when they had sorted out the things they had brought.

'The greengrocer will let me have some boxes,' a girl said. 'He's a friend of my dad's. I'll need some help to carry them, though.'

'Thanks,' Tony said. 'Will you go with her, John, and, perhaps Paul as well? Try to get strong boxes if you can.'

'We could buy some wood, I suppose,' one boy said.

Tony fingered the money in his pocket.

'The less we have to buy the better,' he said. 'Wood is expensive.'

'I thought some of us could go to the library,' Julie suggested. 'We could look at all the books about keeping pets and borrow the best ones. We have five library tickets between us.'

'Good.'

'Then, some of us could find out how much the guinea pigs cost from the pet shop near the cinema,' Julie continued.

'There's another pet shop near the park,' somebody else said. 'We can have a look down there, too.'

'Two of the boys could go along to the builders for the nails and screws,' Tony said. 'Any volunteers?'

Two boys put their hands up.

'We'll go. Give us some money and tell us what you want.'

Tony gave them a pound note and wrote down a list of sizes for the nails.

'Don't forget the change,' he warned. 'We need more nails than screws, I suppose, so just bring twenty screws, an inch long but not too wide.'

One of the boys looked surprised.

'Do they have fat ones and thin ones, then?'

'Of course they do!'

'Who told you?'

'My dad.'

Tony's dad knew all about such matters.

'Well then, let's go,' Julie said. 'Half the morning will be gone if we don't get a move on. There is so much work to do.'

She was hoping to finish at least one hutch so that they could buy a guinea pig. She loved animals.

'Right. Meet at the shed as soon as you can,' Tony said. 'Then we'll make a start on the woodwork.'

They descended on the High Street and went to their separate destinations, to worry the shopkeepers, to beg for boxes, to look at books or simply to compare the prices of the animals. Three of them were thrown out of the library for making too much noise, but, other than that, there were no casualties. Most of them arrived back at the shed within a few minutes of each other.

They worked hard for the rest of the morning, going backwards and forwards every few minutes to borrow a larger hammer or a smaller screwdriver. Or a piece of plaster for a blister or a cut. But it was great fun and, by the time dinner was ready and they rushed off to their homes to tell their parents all they had done, things were definitely taking shape.

'Don't eat so quickly,' Tony's mother said. 'You will have finished your dinner before I had hardly started. What is all the rush for?'

But, of course, she knew and, secretly, she was glad and rather proud like most of the parents of the Cobweb Club children, except she was proudest of all because it was her Tony who had started it.

Tony looked at his mother's plate, which was still three parts covered, and then at his own, which was empty.

'Oh, all right then,' his mother sighed. 'I've put your pudding out in the kitchen. Fetch it, if you want to, and bring mine in, too, while you are about it.'

'Thanks, Mum!'

Tony ate his pudding in one minute.

'Can I go now, please?'

'If you want to, but take care of your father's saw. He won't want that ruined.'

Tony promised to take care of it. When he arrived back at the shed some of the children were there already.

'You shouldn't gobble your food quite so quickly,' Tony said. 'You'll get indigestion!'

Half of them didn't know what that meant.

'I think we'll have lessons in here every morning,' Tony joked. 'Some of you don't know the meaning of simple words.'

They all rushed him and pulled him to the ground.

'I didn't mean it,' he yelled. 'I was only joking!'

They allowed him to get up and he brushed his clothes.

'Serves you right,' Julie laughed. 'Lessons should never be joked about. They will start too soon when we go back to school. Only another four weeks holiday. and then rotten old lessons!'

Towards the end of the afternoon they had made two hutches with proper doors and with wire netting firmly in place. Not all the children had worked on them, some had watched or done other things, experimenting with pieces of wood and sharp, unfamiliar tools. Tony had tried to see that they had all done something useful.

He took out his handkerchief and mopped his brow.

'Phew!'

'You look hot,' Julie said.

'I wish we could have the door open.'

'That's impossible!'

But Tony wasn't so sure. He hoped his letter would do some good and he remembered what Shan had said about seeing the inside of the shed when she walked through the door. She wouldn't climb through the window!

'We still have time to go back to the pet shop and buy the guinea pigs,' a girl suggested, hopefully.

'Yes. Let's!'

The children, and especially the girls, were very

keen to look after animals.

'Yes. Let's,' Julie said.

Julie, too, was becoming quite a leader.

Tony tried to dissuade them.

'It's too late. We aren't really ready yet. We haven't any proper food for them. We don't know enough about them.'

He tried to think of some more reasons, but, each time, they shouted him down.

'We have the library books. We can buy straw and lettuces and collect some grass. There's plenty of water in the tap. We'll manage.'

And Tony knew that they would manage very well.

'Very well,' he relented, taking some more money from the back pocket of his jeans. 'Here, take this. I'll stay and clear up the mess. Don't forget to ask which is the male and the female. It makes a difference, you know.'

Julie looked pained.

'Of course we will, silly. We aren't quite so stupid as you think we are.'

But she only said it in fun. She was too excited to be unkind.

All the other boys went with the girls to the pet shop so Tony was left on his own. He looked around at everything they had done. There was still a lot to do, of course. Something had to done about the rough, cold concrete floor. The walls were badly in need of a coat of paint but, otherwise, things weren't in bad shape. The roof didn't leak, the lights worked and they even had a couple of spare bulbs which his mum had found for him. The hutches looked solid and well made. He decided to move them away from the window opening so they would be out of any draught.

'The sooner that window is put back and we are able to use the door, the better I shall like it,' he said to himself.

He decided on the spot to see Shan about the letter that evening. Then the gang returned.

'They are fab!'

One of the boys had run on ahead to tell Tony. Fab was his in-word. Everything was fab even if it was only a little better than ordinary.

'Oh yes?'

Tony tried to remain casual.

'Come and see.'

Tony scrambled out of the window and met the others as they threaded their way carefully through the estate, followed by some other children who, up to that moment, had not wanted to join the club.

'Look, Tony!'

Julie's eyes sparkled with excitement and pure joy as she held one of the guinea pigs close to her to protect it. Another girl had the other animal, the male.

'Isn't she beautiful?'

Tony nodded.

'She is,' he replied. 'A lovely black, brown and golden colour.'

'With one white foot,' Julie said. 'Look. This one.'

'Let's put them in their hutches before they catch cold,' he suggested. 'They don't like being in the wind.'

'You've been peeping at our library books,' someone said.

Tony hadn't. He had enough common sense to know that all animals prefer the warmth and comfort of a shelter to the wind.

'Here, Julie. I'll hold your guinea pig for you while you climb through,' he offered.

'No, thank you!'

Julie wasn't going to part with her now.

'I'll manage,' she said. 'I want to put her in her new home myself.'

And Tony thought that was fair, for Julie had done most of all the girls to start the Cobweb Club.

'Where's the straw?' he asked. 'And the lettuce leaves and the grass and ...'

'And the water,' somebody said. 'It's all here. We didn't forget anything.'

They placed the straw in each hutch and stuck a tuft of grass through the wire netting. They stood a container of water inside the door.

'It's all ready for them now,' a girl said.

Very gently, Julie put the female guinea pig into one hutch and shut the door. Somebody else put the male into the other hutch. At first, the animals stayed in the darkness of the door section.

'Oh, come out of the bedroom!' Peter said.

Gradually, after a few minutes, two quivering noses appeared and then suddenly, they were both in full view, nibbling at the grass and exploring their cosy corners.

'I think they like our hutches,' Tony said.

'We must be careful not to overfeed them,' Julie warned. 'Shall we make a rota for each week so that we all take a turn at looking after them?'

Everybody thought that was a very good idea.

'I think you girls ought to be in charge of the guinea pigs,' Tony said.

They put the surplus straw into a sack and left it near the hutches.

'Make another rota for cleaning duties,' he said. 'It's important to keep them clean.'

This was agreed.

'Well, we must go now,' he continued. 'And, don't forget, if any of you come back to have a peep at the animals, make sure they are safe in their hutches and that the catch is on before you leave.'

'It would be better not to handle them at all for a few days,' Julie said. 'Then they will have a chance to settle in properly.'

The children were learning to be very sensible.

'Isn't it nice to do things ourselves?' she said later as she walked back through The Flats.

Tony agreed.

'Very nice,' he said. 'But we wouldn't have been able to make the hutches without the tools people have lent us. That was a lovely roll of wire netting Alan brought.'

'His dad gave it to him,' Julie said. 'There's nearly enough left to make a chicken's cage.'

But Tony wasn't having anything to do with that particular brainwave.

'I think we should make a rule that all the animals we keep must be silent ones, or, at least, quiet ones,' he suggested. 'Then the council won't be able to say we are causing trouble.'

Tony was worried about the council. It would be terrible if they were turned out of the shed with so much done and the children's interest running high. He would definitely see Shan after tea. She would know what to do.

When, later, he called on Shan, she was pleased to see him.

'I didn't expect to see you so soon, Tony,' she said. 'Come in.'

He followed her upstairs and into the lounge. He looked around for a few seconds.

'Do you like it, Tony?'

'Oh, yes! Very much!' he replied. 'I like all the ...'

'Muddle?' Shan suggested.

Tony laughed.

'It looks a very organised sort of muddle,' he said. 'You must keep very busy. What is this?'

He pointed to a block of wood with nails sticking out of it. They formed a pattern of brass, new and shiny, like soldiers on parade, evenly spaced and standing up straight.

'That is my picture making corner,' Shan explained. 'I run wire between the nails and make patterns.'

'Did you make that one on the wall?'

It was a picture of a sailing ship.

'Yes. It's not very good, really. It's the first one I made.'

It looked all right to Tony.

'And this is my dressmaking and knitting corner,' Shan continued. 'And, over here, is my nature corner.'

'Like we used to have at school,' Tony said, carefully handling some beautiful shells. 'Did you pick these up off a beach?'

'Yes.'

The rest of the room was littered with books and indoor plants of various shapes and sizes, but, there was an order about everything, Tony thought.

As if Shan sensed what he was thinking she suddenly spoke.

'Believe it or not,' she said. 'I know just where everything is!'

Tony laughed again.

'I don't suppose you waste a minute,' he said.

There was no television in the room.

'Well, I try not to waste very many,' Shan replied.

There was a short silence while Tony wandered around the large room looking at all her things. Shan didn't mind and it seemed natural for Tony to behave in this way. He felt completely at ease with her, a feeling he had never before experienced when in the company of an adult.

'I must tell you why I have come,' he said, suddenly.

Immediately, Shan put down what she was holding, pointed to a chair for him to sit on, and gave him her full attention.

'Fire away,' she said. 'I'm all ears!'

Tony told her about their progress at the club. He told her about his fears for the future, too.

'Will you read your letter to me, please?' Shan said, when he had finished.

She listened carefully.

'It isn't very good, is it?' he said, when he had finished. 'You will have to help me write another one.'

But Shan wouldn't hear of such a suggestion.

'Nonsense!' she said, in her down to earth way. 'It is a very good letter and, most important, it is in your own words. It would be wrong to alter it in any way at all.'

Tony sighed.

'I didn't think it was good enough,' he said.

'There is one thing you will have to alter, though,' Shan said.

'What is that?'

'Our mayor is a lady!'

Tony laughed.

'I didn't know,' he said. 'I'm glad you told me.'

'I think I can tell you where she lives, too,' Shan continued. 'It will be best to send it to her private address. It may get lost in the Town Hall, stuck at the bottom of somebody's in-tray, I shouldn't wonder!'

She walked across to her desk and flicked through some papers.

'Here it is,' she said. 'And here is an envelope and a stamp. If you address it here you can post the letter on your way home.'

'Thank you.'

Shan brushed aside his thanks.

'Anything I can do to help, that is, what you can't do yourself,' she explained. 'Anything you can do, do it, if you see what I mean.'

While Tony sat puzzling out that statement, Shan prepared a fizzy drink.

'Pity you didn't bring Julie with you. I've enough fizzy drink for two. I don't like the stuff myself.'

'Then, why did you buy it?' Tony enquired.

Shan laughed.

'I thought you might call again,' she said.

And that was typical of Shan, Tony thought. She was so different from anybody else he had ever met. He decided to find out why.

'Shan.'

He hesitated.

She handed him his drink in a tall glass.

'Shan.'

'Yes, Tony.'

'Why are you different to all the other grown ups I know? Why do you bother with us kids?'

'I was a kid once,' she said.

'So were all the other grown ups.'

'I have a Friend Who means everything to me.'

'Do I know him?'

'I don't think you do, Tony. I hope you will one day.'

'Is he such a wonderful person? Will you introduce me to him?'

Shan smiled.

'Yes,' she said. 'This Friend, He is also my Leader,' she explained. 'I can't show you a photograph of Him. I can't ask Him to shake your hand. I can't even tell you what He looks like.'

'What?'

Tony was puzzled.

'I can tell you His name,' Shan continued. 'His name is Jesus.'

'Oh, I see,' Tony said, quietly. 'I have heard about Him, of course. At school we used to have stories about Him doing miracles, but we don't have them now. But, He's dead, isn't He? He died on a cross. How can He be your friend?'

Shan smiled.

'It's much more than stories,' she said. 'It is true what you say about Jesus being put to death on a cross. He allowed that to happen to Him so that He could take the punishment for all the sins we have ever done, the wrong things and thoughts. He chose to die for us. He was perfect, the Son of God, Who loves me and you and wants to lead us in His way. God raised Him from the dead to prove that Jesus really was His Son. So, He is still alive and always will be!'

Tony looked doubtful.

'If He's alive, He must live somewhere,' he said. 'Where does He live?'

'He lives in Heaven and in my heart,' Shan said.

Tony caught his breath and sat up straight.

'And that is why you are different,' he said.

'I hope so,' Shan replied.

Tony looked down at his feet. Suddenly, he wanted to leave, to go home. He wasn't ready to take in any more shocks. So he got up and put his tall glass on the table.

'I think I'll go home now,' he said, quietly. 'But I'll come again and you can tell me more.'

Shan smiled, warmly.

'Yes,' she said. You need a Leader, too. Don't forget to post your letter.'

'I won't forget to post it,' Tony said. 'But I shall be surprised if the mayor takes much notice of it.'

Shan smiled again.

'Don't be too surprised if she does. Remember, I have a Leader Who can still do miracles. And He knows about your Cobweb Club, too!'

CHAPTER SEVEN

TURNED OUT

Tony posted the letter on his way home. He was deep in thought and not paying any attention to the other people who were walking along the street when he heard a familiar voice.

'Hi, Tony!'

Tony swung round. It was Mr Monsingh, the foreign gentleman, whose car they had cleaned.

'Oh, hello!'

Tony was alert again.

'It looked as if you were miles away in your thoughts,' the man laughed. 'Can you spare a minute? I have something to show you that might be of interest to you.'

Tony was curious.

'Of interest to me? I wonder what it can be?'

Mr Monsingh laughed again and Tony thought how happy he seemed.

'Don't get too excited,' he said. 'You might not like it.'

They soon came to the big house with the bells.

'Wait here, please,' he said to Tony. 'I'll go and find it.'

Tony waited. Soon he heard the man coming down-stairs. Through the half open door Tony saw that he was carrying a large piece of wood. A chain was hanging loose.

'There!' he said as he put the wood down. 'It really is quite heavy, but I shall help you to carry it home, that is, if you will accept it.'

He turned the wood around.

'Oh! That's ...'

Tony struggled to find the right word.

'That's perfect!'

Mr Monsingh smiled with pleasure.

'Not perfect,' he said. 'It is only my humble effort but I hoped you might be pleased.'

'Pleased! You wait until the others see it! You will be our friend for life!'

Mr Monsingh beamed.

'It is always good to be friends,' he replied.

Tony looked closely at the wood. It really was a work of great beauty. The painting had been worked in oils and showed a delicate curtain of cobwebs draping a window through which the sun was trying to shine. Over the top of the picture were the words, 'The Cobweb Club.' Standing, one on either side of of the window, were a boy and a girl. Tony and Julie!

'It's beautiful! It's really beautiful!'

Tony felt completely stunned. Why should this man be so kind? The painting must have taken hours of work. Suddenly, he had a thought; an important thought. He knew he had to ask a question, just as he had asked Shan. He looked straight into the man's eyes.

'Is Jesus your friend, too?'

The eyes came alive with light. Tony knew the answer before he heard it.

'Yes. I am a Christian. I am a follower of Jesus Christ. Tell me, is He your Leader, too?'

The question was asked with great kindness. Tony shook his head a little and clutched the wood.

'No,' he sighed.

He was beginning to wish he could have said, 'Yes.'

'No. But another person who lives near here has been as kind as you. And she is a Christian. She has the same warm smile that you have. I just knew you must follow Jesus as well.'

The foreign gentleman looked thoughtful.

'It is nice to hear you say that,' he said. 'You are indeed fortunate to meet two Christians out of all the people living in this area. God must have planned it for your good. But it isn't any credit to me. If Jesus lives in my heart you ought to be able to see Him in my face.'

'And in what you do,' Tony said.

'Of course! But you must also remember that there are many kind people who are not Christians, too.'

Tony nodded.

'I think I understand,' he said. 'But it's strange you used the same word as my other friend. She said I needed a leader, too.'

'And she is quite right. Listen carefully to what she tells you.'

They carried the painting along the street and down the hill to The Flats. A handful of children ran towards them.

'Looks as though you have plenty of help now,' Mr Monsingh said.

They rested the wood on the wall by the side of the pavement.

'Thank you again, Mr ...'

Tony's sentence tailed off, unfinished.

'My friends call me Abdul.'

Tony smiled. He had found another friend.

'Thank you, Abdul.'

Tony extended his hand and Abdul took it.

'Look after the painting, Tony,' he said.

But he knew his words were unnecessary. He turned and walked off up the hill.

'Did he paint that?' the other children asked.

Tony and another boy held the painting so everybody could see it clearly.

'It's great!'

They were all in agreement.

'I'm going to keep it at home until it can be hung up properly,' Tony said. 'One day we shall hang it over the door.'

They walked with Tony to his block and helped him carry the painting up the stairs.

'Thanks. I can manage now. Will one of you knock on Julie's door? I want her to see it before she goes to bed. She knows the man who painted it.'

Tony took the painting indoors and showed it to his parents.

'My! You are doing well!' his dad said. 'That is what I call a real work of art.'

Tony's mother laughed.

'What do you know about real works of art?' she teased. 'Oh, but it is beautiful. Very beautiful.'

Then Julie arrived.

'You'll catch your death!' Tony's mother said, looking at Julie's bare feet and flimsy nightdress. 'Do that dressing gown up, my girl.'

Tony's mother had a powerful voice when she wanted to be firm.

'Sorry. But I was just getting into bed.'

She turned to Tony.

'Well, don't keep me waiting. Show it to me,' she demanded.

Tony's father grinned and picked up his evening paper again. He was very fond of his papers.

'Another sergeant major in the making,' he muttered.

Tony's mother gave him a withering look.

'Come along, Julie,' Tony said, wisely. 'We have put the painting in my bedroom.'

Afterwards, when the flat was quiet and Julie had long since gone home, Tony lay staring at the painting in his bedroom.

'It's great!' he kept saying to himself.

When, finally, he switched off his light and went to sleep, he had a dream; a strange dream. There was a great army of people, men and women, boys and girls, marching along behind a leader whose face he could not see. They were all singing and they looked so happy that Tony wished he were marching with them. He saw Shan and Abdul, faces aglow, eyes shining brightly, and a host of other people from all over the world, but, though he looked eagerly, he did not see himself. The crowd marched on into the sunlight and he stood just watching them pass. Suddenly, and with a start, he awoke.

'Come on, Tony, it's morning!' his mother was saying.

So he never finished his dream and he never saw the leader's face, but he thought he knew who the leader was. He thought it was The Leader. Jesus.

After breakfast he walked round to the shed. The girls were already there. The guinea pigs seemed to be enjoying all the attention.

'When can we make some more hutches?' Julie asked. 'We could have dozens of guinea pigs then.'

'We might be able to make another two today,' Tony said. 'Wood isn't cheap and we shall probably have to buy what we need. We can't expect the greengrocer to give us too many boxes. We have spent over half our money already.'

'We can't wash any more cars just yet,' Julie said. 'They won't be dirty, will they? Can't we think of some other idea?'

But they couldn't. Washing cars seemed to be the best.

'Perhaps some of the people who wouldn't let us work for them will hear how well we did the other cars,' Tony suggested. 'But, there is still quite a lot of work to do here, in the shed. We ought to make it as nice as we can. The council may come to see what we are doing.'

'Did you write to them, then?'

Julie looked quite fierce.

'Yes,' he admitted.

He must have had a guilty look on his face.

'You didn't post it!'

Tony nodded.

'But, Tony! You promised to show it to us!'

Julie was very upset.

'I'm sorry, Julie, I really am. I quite forgot about my promise when I posted the letter. Anyway, how did you know I would write to the council? I didn't tell you who I was going to write to.'

'You didn't have to. I guessed.'

Julie seemed satisfied with his apology. The others were still fondling the guinea pigs to be much concerned.

'I'll read what I wrote,' he said, by way of a peace offering.

He pulled the copy of his letter from his pocket and they all gathered round.

'It's quite good,' Julie admitted, when he had finished.

The others agreed.

'I hope they don't charge too much for the window,' somebody said. 'Especially as Tony is paying for it.'

'Oh, that's not fair!' Julie protested.

She was back on his side.

'We'll all help to pay for it. Won't it be great when they unlock the door and we can hang up our sign for everybody to see!'

Tony grinned.

'I only hope it all comes true,' he said.

Most of the boys arrived soon after and Tony explained what he had done. They thought he was mad.

'They are bound to kick us out!' one said.

'We shall have done all this hard work for nothing.'

'It's no use writing to the mayor. He will be too busy to take any notice. Besides, we are only a bunch of kids. He won't listen to us.'

'It's a she not a he,' Tony said, miserably. 'Perhaps everything will work out right in the end.'

In the early afternoon his hopes were quickly dashed. They had spent the entire morning working hard. The girls had tended the animals. It was a warm,

lazy sort of day and Tony was doing nothing in particular, fingering his mouth organ and looking out
into the haze towards the wooded, wealthy area across
the valley. Suddenly, he heard a commotion and the
sounds of running feet, many feet, like a pack of
hounds. The gang rounded the corner at full speed.

'Now what's the matter!'

Tony knew something was badly wrong.

'The shed!'

'The council!'

'The workmen!'

'Boarding up!'

'Big planks and long nails!'

'What about the guinea pigs?'

'They'll die!'

Tony heard it all at once from a dozen voices.

'Come and see for yourself. Quick!'

But he didn't need any urging. He shot around the
corner and streaked across the balding grass before
they had recovered their breath and had started to
stumble after him.

'Hi!'

Tony shouted.

'Hi!'

A couple of solid looking workmen in blue overalls
were carrying heavy planks behind the shed. They
hardly looked up when Tony called.

'That's our shed!' Tony exclaimed, when he
reached them. 'What are you doing with those
planks?'

One of the men turned around, leaned his plank
against the shed wall and pushed his cap further back
on his head. A train went by.

'Your shed?'

The man wasn't mocking Tony. He wasn't being unkind. He was just curious.

By this time the other children had arrived and they stood behind Tony in a group.

'Your shed?'

'Yes, well, no.'

Tony didn't know what to say.

The man looked at his mate and then at his watch.

'Now, what is all this fuss about?' he asked. 'Hurry up and explain. We have to do another three jobs after this one.'

'We use the shed for our club,' Tony explained. 'It all began when I broke the window by accident. Then we looked inside, saw that it was nearly empty and decided we would clean it and use the shed for ourselves.'

'Did you now,' the man said. 'And who gave you permission to take over council property without so much as a by your leave?'

'It wasn't being used,' Julie said. 'It was just standing there. We didn't do any harm.'

Tony was very anxious. The men looked solid and unmoved, good servants of the council who paid their wages.

'Can't you leave the window for a few more days? Please!'

The men shook their heads.

'Sorry, son, and all of you. But, no. Orders are orders. We've come along to board up the window and that's what we intend to do, club or no club.'

'Who told you it was broken?'

'I bet it was old Mrs Pinkham,' somebody else said.

'I'll smash her window for her. That'll teach her to be so nosey.'

'Shoosh!'

Tony tried to quieten them.

'Shoosh! That sort of talk won't do any good,' he said.

'I don't know who told the council,' the foreman said. 'It might have been somebody who was on a passing train and not anybody from the estate. And I shouldn't let your gang go around smashing windows.'

The foreman looked very serious.

'That will only make matters worse,' he said.

'But, what about the guinea pigs?' Julie said. 'Where can we put them? We aren't allowed to have them indoors. It's against the rules.'

The foreman thought for a minute.

'They won't come to any harm if you leave them outside,' he said. 'It is going to be a warm, fine night. Give them some extra straw and they will be quite happy. Perhaps the council will let you use the shed if you ask them nicely.'

'I have asked them,' Tony said. 'Well, not the council.'

'He wrote to the mayor,' Julie said, proudly. 'You'll get into awful trouble if you nail up that window!'

But it was no use. Not until the men wanted to use their hammer. They couldn't find it anywhere.

'Did you leave it on the van, Fred?' the foreman asked.

'I'm sure I didn't.'

'Well, it's not here, is it? Run back and have a look. I expect it's with the other things.'

But it wasn't.

'Now, look here!'

The foreman was beginning to look stern.

'The person who has taken that hammer will give it back to me. Now!'

He stood waiting, his hands on his hips, like Tony's mum when she was cross.

'Give it back,' Tony said, not knowing who had taken it.

Slowly, Julie pulled it from behind her back. She was very near to tears.

'It isn't fair,' she sobbed. 'I think you're horrible!'

Tony tried to comfort her.

'It isn't any use crying,' he said. 'The workmen have to do their job, otherwise they will get into trouble.'

'That's quite right, son,' the foreman said. 'I expect it will all come right in the end if you have written to the mayor. She is very nice.'

'I hope you're right,' Tony said. 'And I am sorry about the hammer but Julie was upset. The animals mean a lot to her.'

The foreman nodded.

'Well, we can give a helping hand with them,' he said. 'I think we can just squeeze the hutches past the wire if I bend it back a little.'

They managed very well.

'Did you make these?' the men asked Tony when they had stood the hutches carefully on the ground.

'Yes. But we all helped.'

The foreman looked around the group.

'How many of you do woodwork at school?' he asked.

Most of them weren't old enough. Only Tony.

'Well, you have made a good job of these, son. Might

be a job for you with the council one day if you can turn out good work like this already. How old are you?'

'I'm nearly twelve.'

'Starting a new school after the holidays?'

'Yes.'

'Which one?'

'Forest Road.'

'Good. They have a first class workshop there. And a good teacher. You'll learn fast.'

Tony was beginning to like the foreman.

'Well, come on, Fred. We'll leave the children to carry the hutches to the shelter of the back wall. Let's get this job over and done with.'

They soon boarded up the window and made ready to go.

'If you get a message to come and unboard it, will you come back straight away?' Tony asked.

'Straight away,' the foreman promised. 'Mind you, you should have asked permission, but you've done very well with the woodwork. I'll have a word with the superintendent of works first thing tomorrow morning. Perhaps he will be able to do something to help.'

'Oh, would you? Thanks.'

'Goodbye then.'

'I knew it wouldn't last,' Julie said, bitterly, as they watched the men drive away. 'It was too good to be true. Nobody cares about kids!'

CHAPTER EIGHT

TONY READS A BOOK

Tony's parents were furious when he told them what had happened.

'It's a terrible shame,' his mother said.

She nudged Tony's father.

'Can't you do something about it?'

'I suppose I could try,' he said, slowly. 'But we don't want to get into trouble with the council. It's different for the kids. They can get away with almost anything these days. Besides, they don't have to pay the rent.'

'But what can a crowd of children do?' Tony's mother continued. 'They haven't anybody to speak up for them.'

Tony smiled to himself. At least his parents were united about the shed. So often they argued about things.

'Don't worry,' he said, cheerfully. 'I expect we'll think of something. The workman said he would tell the superintendent of works about us. He sounds a very important man.'

'Probably sits around all day, drinking tea,' his father scoffed. 'Money for jam I say!'

'Did you write to the council like you said you would?'

Tony looked at his mother closely.

'You knew I was going to, didn't you!'

She smiled.

'It's easy to see where you get your determination from,' she said.

'That's right,' Tony's father said. 'You get it from me, of course!'

'If you were a little more determined we wouldn't have to put up with the squeaky swings,' she laughed. 'No, Tony. You get all your pluck from me.'

'I did better than write to the council,' Tony said, enjoying their good humoured banter. 'I posted my letter last night. I wrote to the mayor.'

Tony's mother looked amazed. His father nearly dropped his pipe. He was so surprised.

'Good for you, Tony,' he said, when he had recovered. 'Now, that's what I call enterprise. But, how did you know where he lives?'

'The mayor is a lady,' Tony said. 'And I have a friend who knows nearly everything.'

His father grinned and pointed his pipe at him.

'Then you'll be top of your class next term. If you don't know what to do, just ask this friend, whatever his name is!'

'It's not a him,' Tony said, under his breath.

He coughed.

'Perhaps I will,' he continued, out loud. 'Yes, that's a very good idea.'

Tony wandered around the estate before making up his mind about going to see Shan. He felt he ought to try to sort things out for himself but, somehow, he couldn't see quite what to do. He could still remember the address on the envelope so he could call on the mayor, but it would take a lot of courage and, probably, she wouldn't be too pleased to see him. He

had a peep at the guinea pigs. They were quite comfortable and wouldn't come to any harm. So, why not
wait until tomorrow? He kicked at a piece of paper
someone had thrown down. The act reminded him of
the old tin can that had started it all.

'No. I'll see Shan tonight,' he said, out loud. 'She
will know what to do.'

Fortunately, Shan had just arrived home when he
rang her bell.

'I'm sorry to worry you again,' he began.

Shan smiled.

'It must be important,' she said. 'Come on in. I can
spare you a little while then I have to go out again.'

He followed her upstairs and they went into her
kitchen.

'Have you had your tea, Tony?'

He nodded.

'Yes, thank you.'

'Sit down, then, while I make myself some coffee
and have a bite to eat. You can tell me about it while
I am doing the toast.'

So Tony told her. She didn't interrupt.

'Well, what do you think?' he asked, when he had
finished his story.

Shan chewed away at her toast and had a drink before answering.

'I think you have done well,' she said. 'You have
written to the mayor. You have put all the animals in
a safe place. You have made a friend of the foreman
who is going to tell the big boss at the Town Hall
about your problem.'

Tony looked puzzled.

'So, what do I do next?' he asked.

'Nothing! Nothing at all! Just wait and see. I think some good will come out of all this. Probably sooner than you dare to hope.'

'But we can't use the shed!'

'So what? You can't use the shed, perhaps for two or three days. Does that matter so much? Now, Tony! Don't start feeling sorry for yourself! You will make everybody else unhappy too. Remember, you are the leader of the club.'

Tony sighed.

'I'm not much of a leader,' he said. 'I wish I could hand over to somebody else.'

Shan smiled.

'Perhaps, one day soon, you will realise that you can,' she said, warmly. 'None of us can cope with everything. There are all sorts of worries and troubles. That's why it is important to have a friend like I have.'

'Jesus?'

'Yes.'

'I think I dreamed about him last night.'

'Did you?'

It was Shan's turn to be surprised.

'Do you want to tell me about it?'

'Yes.'

So Tony told her about his dream and about Abdul too; about the wonderful painting and about Abdul also being a follower of Jesus.

'I never knew there were so many Christians around this area,' he said.

Shan laughed.

'You are learning a lot in a short time, Tony. I don't know Abdul but I should certainly like to meet him. He sounds nice. There aren't as many of us as there ought to be but, perhaps, that is our fault. We don't talk about Jesus as much as we should. But, I think there are Christians in every country in the world.'

'So, my dream was true, in a way,' he said. 'There were people from every country marching along, all sorts of colours and different clothes. Some had hardly any clothes at all. But they all looked so happy.'

Shan smiled again.

'And you were there!' he continued. 'You and Abdul. I saw you ever so clearly.'

Shan rinsed her coffee cup under the tap and put it with her plate in the washing up bowl.

'Tony. I'm going to turn you out now,' she said, quite suddenly. 'I have to go right away. It's very important.'

Tony rose from his chair.

'I'm going to give you a little book to read,' she continued. 'It's all words of Jesus. Words He spoke when He was on earth.'

She went to her cupboard and rummaged through a small pile of books.

'Here,' she said at last. 'This is the one.'

Tony took it and put it in his pocket.

'I don't read books very often,' he said. 'But, I'll read this one. I'll read it all.'

Shan smiled.

'Good. It won't take you more than twenty minutes to read. I'll think of you reading it.'

'Will you really?'

'Yes. I promise.'

She showed him to the door and, once again, they parted; Tony back to The Flats; Shan to prepare for her errand. Somehow, Tony's problem about know-

ing what to do for the best seemed smaller, if not un-
important, compared with his desire to know more
about this leader. He fingered the book in his pocket.
He would read it as soon as he could. After all, if they
were the words of Jesus, he must give them all his
attention.

Three of the club members passed him when he
reached the estate.

'Hiya Tone!'

'Hiya.'

'The animals are all right. We've just had a look.'

'Good. See you tomorrow.'

Tony felt much happier. For once, he couldn't wait
to go to bed. He wanted to read his little book in
private but his mother insisted that he must eat his
supper.

'You must have a wash, too,' she said, firmly.

'Oh, all right. But, I'm not really dirty.'

She looked at him closely.

'Do you feel well, son? It's at least an hour before
your usual bedtime.'

'I'm fine, mum. I think I'll have an early night,
though. It's been a long day.'

He stretched his arms wide and yawned.

'Besides,' he continued. 'You and dad can watch
the telly in peace.'

The book was interesting. He had heard about
Jesus, of course. Jesus was a figure in history like anybody else who had lived long ago. He had heard about
the miracles Jesus was supposed to have done, how he
made blind men see and lame men walk. He knew
Jesus was supposed to have walked on the sea. That
was a bit far fetched, he thought! But, he had never

thought how somebody who had lived so long ago could matter now. He had never thought about Jesus coming alive again. He knew about the cross, of course. Nearly everybody knew about the cross; about Jesus being crucified by the Romans with the help of some who should have realised that Jesus was very special, but were blinded by their own jealousy. But, coming alive again! That proved that Jesus was special!

Tony read on, eagerly.

'And Jesus told his disciples it would happen and even they were slow to take it in! It was so big! So tremendous!'

Tony spoke quietly to himself, shifted his position on the bed and read as fast as he could. In his heart he knew that what he was reading was the truth, because he had met Abdul and Shan; because of all those other people he had met in his dream.

He put the book down when he had finished it, switched off his bedside light and lay thinking. Abdul's painting was propped against the opposite wall and he could just see the details in the semi-darkness.

'One day, perhaps, I shall be like them,' he said, thinking of his new found friends and not considering that Jesus wanted him to be like them now.

In the morning Tony waited for the postman. When he brought two letters Tony had a sudden, excited feeling that one of them was for him, but it wasn't.

'You won't hear from the council as quickly as that,' his mother said. 'They take a week to think about anything, then they have to find a typist who is willing to do some work.'

Tony's mother hadn't a very high opinion of the council and he was surprised that she didn't say also that they weren't quite so slow about coming to collect the rent, like she usually said. But, this time, she didn't.

It was a dreary sort of morning; not that the sun wasn't shining, but there just didn't seem much to do.

'What did we used to do before we took over the shed?' he asked Julie, who was hanging around the hutches looking so miserable that Tony said she seemed to have gone into a black cloud.

'We used to waste all our time in the playground, that's what!' Julie retorted, looking like an old cross-patch. 'Wasn't much use writing to the mayor, was it? She's not interested in us.'

Tony tried to think of something cheerful to say.

'Perhaps a letter will come by the midday post,' he suggested, not really believing it would.

'Perhaps!' Julie snorted, like a miniature pig. 'Perhaps! It was always perhaps!'

She was ever so angry and near to tears. Tony started to say that perhaps something would turn up but he stopped himself in time.

'Something will turn up,' he said, firmly, leaving out the perhaps. 'I know it will!'

And he meant what he said. He had no idea why, or how, unless it was something to do with the little book he had read, but, quite rightly, he knew that he was not all on his own. Without knowing it, he was entering the world of Shan and Abdul; the world of hope, and faith, and expecting God to do something, although he couldn't have put this into words.

'Well, it had better!' Julie said, darkly. 'Otherwise...'

It was one of her longest words and she liked it. It had an air of mystery; of threatening.

'Otherwise...'

'Otherwise, what?'

She thought for a moment and a mischievous grin spread slowly across her face.

'Otherwise, I'll smash the other window and we'll move in again.'

But Tony knew she didn't mean it. It was her own way of relieving her anger and disappointment.

'How are the guinea pigs?' he enquired, changing the subject to her favourite topic.

'Oh, they are all right, I suppose,' she drawled. 'If they had been in the shed we could have put them together and they might have started a family, then we should have some more to look after.'

Tony grinned.

'Then we should need some more hutches. We haven't very much money left for wood. It costs such a lot.'

'We can clean some more cars on Saturday,' she suggested. 'Abdul will give us some money. He's great, isn't he?'

Tony looked doubtful.

'Abdul has already given us far more than we deserve,' he reminded her. 'So has Shan, not so much in things, but advice.'

'Which has got us nowhere!' Julie retorted, still feeling fed up.

'Oh, no! That's not fair,' Tony said. 'Something

will turn up. You'll see.'

Tony walked away from Julie and left her to tend to the animals. He felt inclined to be cross with her, but she was younger than himself and it was easy to excuse her bad behaviour. She had been a great help in starting the club. She had worked very hard. He understood how badly she felt now.

The postman didn't call at midday. For a moment Tony felt, perhaps, he would never come, but he shook off this feeling as a dog shakes off water from an unwanted dip in a cold pond. He strode to his room, found the little book and opened it again.

'If you ask anything in My Name, I will do it.'

The golden words seemed to stand out from the page. Very quietly, not above a whisper, Tony decided to put Jesus to the test.

'Please, Jesus. Make something good happen soon.'

That was all he said. That was his first prayer. He didn't even mention the shed or the council or anything else. But, in his heart, he knew Jesus had heard and understood. He had handed over his problem to someone he couldn't see.

After tea a van drew up by the estate. Tony saw it from the balcony where he was loitering, looking at the buildings in Central London. A thick set man in blue climbed slowly out and made his unhurried way through the estate. Tony shot downstairs like a rocket in reverse!

'I've got something for you, young man,' the fore-man said. 'Here! Catch this!'

Something glinted in the evening sun and Tony caught it with one hand.

'A key!' he exclaimed.

'Not just a key!' the foreman said. 'The key! The key to the shed. Your shed!'

Tony clasped it in both hands until the metal felt warm. He was lost for words. And very happy.

'Well? Do you want a hand to move the animals back?' the foreman asked. 'Or would you rather ask your young friends to help?'

Tony found his voice at last.

'We can do it,' he said. 'That is, if you don't mind. But, the key? Can we keep it?'

The foreman smiled.

Yes. You are responsible for it,' he said. 'And, you'll be hearing from the council in due course. I'll come and unboard the window and put some new glass in it tomorrow morning.'

He turned to go, chuckling to himself.

'When did you know about all this?' Tony asked.

'Just after midday. I would have come before but I was working on another estate. I called here on my way home.'

'Thank you ever so much,' Tony said, only restraining himself from hugging the foreman with great difficulty. 'Can I help you with the window in the morning?'

The foreman smiled.

'All right,' he said. 'I'll show you how to put glass in the proper way.'

Tony clutched the key and watched him go.

'It must have happened at the same time I asked Jesus,' he said.

From that moment, Tony knew that, one day, Jesus

would be his Leader, too.

But, right now, he had to tell the others about the key.

CHAPTER NINE

THE PROPER WAY

Tony ran round to the back of the estate. Most of the gang were near the hutches.

'Tony looks excited!'

Julie dropped the straw she was holding and turned to greet him.

'Have you heard from the mayor?' she asked.

Tony shook his head.

'No,' he replied, keeping them in suspense. 'No, I haven't heard from the mayor yet, but ...'

'But, what?'

They spoke together, with one voice.

A grin split Tony's face from ear to ear.

'I've got the key of the door,' he sang.

'Where?'

'Here!'

Tony unscrewed his fingers and showed them the hot palm of his left hand.

'Here!'

'How did you get it?'

'The foreman brought it.'

'I knew he was on our side really,' somebody said. 'He was upset about moving the animals out and boarding up the window.'

Tony nodded.

'He saw the superintendent of works,' he explained.

'Just like he promised. The key is ours! We can go in the proper way!'

'And nobody will stop us!' Julie exclaimed.

She did a leap in the air which made her flimsy dress whirl like a wheel.

'Well? What are we waiting for?' she asked, when she had picked herself off the ground.

'Yes. What are we waiting for?' Tony repeated. 'Let's move all these hutches back inside.'

The good news spread quickly. Before they had staggered across the tarmac with the hutches all the other members of the Cobweb Club and a few others, including some mums and dads, had arrived on the scene. Everybody seemed to be excited. And happy!

'You must go in first,' Julie said.

Tony put the key in the lock. He fumbled with it.

'It might need a drop of oil,' somebody suggested.

But it didn't. They watched anxiously to see if it would really fit and, when it turned and Tony opened the door, a great cheer went up which must have been heard by everybody in The Flats.

Tony stood aside and let the others rush in before him. Julie protested loudly.

'Hey!' she shouted. 'You should have gone in first!'

He laughed.

'It doesn't matter who goes in first,' he said. 'We can go in, all of us. That is what matters.'

Julie agreed.

'You said things would come out right in the end and they did.'

'We have to thank the foreman,' Tony replied. 'He came specially in his van on his way home from work. He knew we would be pleased. He's coming again

tomorrow to put new glass in the window so it will
be light in here again.'

Julie looked very guilty.

'I'm sorry I took his hammer,' she said. 'I did get
rather cross with him.'

'Rather!' Tony replied. 'Never mind. I'm sure he
knew how upset you were, and all of us, too.'

The children chattered noisily in the shed. The
parents went back, smiling, to their chores.

'I think the guinea pigs know they are back in their
home,' Tony said.

'We must leave them now. We musn't get them
too excited.'

Julie adored the animals and she steered the others
away from the hutches towards the door.

'We can come back in the morning,' she explained.
'They will have had time to settle down again by
then.'

'I'll keep the key,' Tony said, when they had locked
the door behind them. 'Don't let's come into the shed
tomorrow until the window is fixed, except for me, of
course. I'm going to help the foreman.'

'Lucky you,' Julie said. 'But, that's a good idea. The
foreman won't want a crowd of us getting in his way.
I don't suppose it will take very long to fix. Not with
your help!'

Tony pushed her.

'Cheeky!' he said. 'He is going to show me how to
do it. I'm not an expert.'

Next morning, at nine o'clock, the little van drew
up at the kerbside with the sheet of glass and other
odds and ends loaded on the back.

Tony, who had been waiting twenty minutes for it

to arrive, was on the spot instantly.

'Thought I'd come to meet you,' he explained. 'Thought I might carry something for you.'

The foreman smiled.

'And so you can,' he said. 'Here. Take the tool box. Careful. It's rather heavy. I'll bring the glass.'

Tony took the tool box with both hands and nearly dropped it. The foreman laughed.

'I told you it was heavy,' he said. 'Are you sure you can carry it?'

Tony nodded.

'Of course I can!'

He staggered after the foreman, pausing to rest several times on the way. He was glad when they reached the shed.

'Phew!' he said, putting the box down carefully. 'I wouldn't like to carry that very far!'

'I'll let you open the door,' the foreman said. 'Then I can take the glass straight inside without resting it. It doesn't help to put glass on a hard floor more than is necessary. Tends to chip easily.'

Tony inserted his key into the lock. This time it turned easily. Before they started work he showed the foreman all they had done so far. They had a look at the animals, too.

'What do you think of the shed?' Tony asked. 'We haven't finished it yet, of course.'

'I think you have all done very well. The old place looks as though it has taken on a new lease of life. Smelt a bit musty before.'

Tony laughed.

'We used rather a lot of disinfectant first of all,' he admitted. 'One of the girls said it smelt like a hospital.'

The foreman grinned.

'Well, you must have worked hard. And I'm sure you enjoyed doing it, didn't you?'

Tony had to agree.

'We did, very much. And we thought it was all about to fizzle out, just like a damp firework.'

'I'm glad it didn't,' the foreman said. 'It's much better to have something to build than something to break. I hope they let you stay here for a long time.'

'Do you think they will?'

'Yes. You wouldn't have got the key otherwise.'

They set to work. First they removed the planks from the window. As they were nailed from the outside the foreman was able to hammer them out with hefty blows of his big hammer. Tony climbed through the space and put the wood in a tidy pile by the wire. Then the foreman started to remove little fragments of glass with his knife.

'I thought I had taken all the glass out,' Tony said, as the foreman kept on discovering bits that had been missed.

'The secret of putting glass in properly is to make sure the framework is cleaned first,' the foreman explained. 'All this loose putty has to come out and in it are embedded the nails that hold the glass in place. Hand me the pliers, please.'

Tony did as he was asked.

'Jesus was a carpenter, wasn't He?' Tony said, suddenly.

The foreman paused in his task.

'What made you say that, son?' he asked.

Tony blushed.

'I don't know really,' he said. 'It just came out. I've

been reading about Jesus lately and I think He helped me to believe everything would come right in the end, about the shed I mean.'

'Did He now? That's very interesting. Strange how people seem so shy of talking about Jesus, don't you think? I've known Him since I was about your age.'

'So you are a Christian, too?'

'Yes. I am. Mind you, I was a real tearaway when I was a lad. God had a big struggle with me. You see, son, there's a war going on inside us all, although some seem not to notice because they have given up, I suppose. Surrendered to the wrong side.'

'A war?'

The foreman removed the last piece of putty and started to brush the framework with a stiff brush.

'Now for the paint,' he said.

Tony handed him another brush and a pot of white paint. The foreman painted the frame carefully.

'The paint makes the new putty stick better,' he explained.

Tony was learning all the time.

'Don't you think there's a war on then, son?'

Tony thought hard.

'I think I know what you mean about a war,' he replied. 'Sometimes you hear a little voice speaking to you right down inside.'

The foreman turned.

'Really,' he said. 'What sort of voice do you mean? Like mine, perhaps.'

'No, not your sort of voice,' Tony said. 'It's hard to explain, really. But, if I see a nice juicy apple hanging over somebody's wall, within reach, the first thing I think of is to pick it, just as if somebody had told me

to, deep down inside. Then, right away, I hear another voice which tells me not to pick the apple, because it's wrong. Is that what you mean?'

'Exactly!' the foreman said. 'That's what I mean
when I say there is a war on. You want to do good
but a voice tells you to do bad things.'

'Sometimes I want to do bad things,' Tony admitted. 'And a voice tells me not to.'

'Then that is the voice of God,' the foreman said.
'He hates all wrong and loves what is pure, honest and
true.'

'You sound just like Shan,' Tony said. 'She's a
Christian, too. And, I have another Christian friend
called Abdul, though he doesn't talk so much as Shan.
He does things instead. Good things.'

They puttied the window. Tony did the lower part
while the foreman guided his hands and made sure
he used the right amount.

'Good. That looks just right,' he said. 'Now we can
press the edge of the glass gently on to the putty and
secure it with the nails.'

Tony shook his head.

'You must put the nails in,' he said. 'I shall probably put the hammer through the glass and we shall
have to start all over again.'

The foreman smiled.

'All right,' he said. 'I'll do it.'

Tony watched.

'There. That will do.'

The foreman stood back and wiped his hands on a
piece of cloth.

'Now we have to put in some more putty round the
glass, level it off and then pack up. There are three

more jobs waiting for me before lunch.'

They hurried on with the work and, in next to no time, everything was completed.

'Well. That's another job done,' the foreman said.

'Thank you for letting me help you. And thank you for being so kind. I'll remember about the war and about listening to the right voice. I want to do what is right. It's much better.'

The foreman nodded.

'When I know I am obeying God's voice,' he said, 'then I am happy. You want to be happy, don't you, son?'

'Yes. Since I met Shan and Abdul and, now, you, I have learned a lot. I didn't know there were so many Christians around.'

'Not half as many as there should be. Have another chat to Shan about your little book. She will put you on the right road. I think I know Shan myself.'

Tony looked surprised.

'Do you go to the same church then?' he asked.

The foreman smiled.

'No, actually I don't. I go to another church quite near here.'

'Then, how do you ...'

'How do I know her?'

'Yes.'

'She's my little girl,' the foreman said. 'Least, she was once. She grew up too fast. I'm her dad!'

When they emerged from the shed into the sunlight, a reception committee awaited them. Julie had all the gang lined up on the grass.

'We wanted to buy you a present,' she said, stepping forward to present the foreman with a big bag of sweets. 'It's from all of us.'

The workman looked into her face and then into the paper bag.

'Bullseyes!' he exclaimed. 'They are my favourites! You must have known!'

Julie beamed with pleasure.

'That's good,' she said. 'We bought them ourselves and we hope you will enjoy them. And. And, I'm sorry I took your hammer.'

She wasn't used to making speeches.

'Thank you very much, Julie, and all of you.'

The foreman put his arm around her and kissed her on the forehead.

'It's all right about the hammer!' he whispered into her ear.

'You must come back and see our club when it is in full swing,' Tony said.

'Thank you, Tony. I shall look forward to that. Look after the animals, all of you. And keep up the good work.'

They escorted him to his van.

'Don't forget what I said now,' the foreman whispered to Tony, before climbing into the driving seat. 'It's very important to obey the right voice. But, see Shan. She will explain things better than I can.'

'I will. Goodbye.'

'Goodbye all.'

The van went down the hill towards the shops.

'Come in and see the window,' Tony said.

They did.

'It's nice, isn't it?' Julie said. 'Did he really let you help?'

'Yes. He did. But I wouldn't like to knock the nails

in. They are too close to the glass.'

Julie looked closely at the window.

'I can't see any nails. Where are they?'

'Underneath the putty. You can't see them but they are there all right. Otherwise the glass wouldn't stay in.'

'And we don't want it to fall out again, do we?' Alan said.

'What shall we do now?' Julie asked.

Tony thought hard for a minute.

'I think we should have a full meeting of the club members,' he suggested. 'Things are different now. We have a key. The window is mended.'

'And the council know we are here,' Julie interrupted.

'Yes. So, let's round up all our members and meet back here in ten minutes. It's time we decided our next step.'

The other members of the club were soon found as well as some newcomers who said they wanted to join. They made a list of things they wanted to do and another list of what was needed.

'What we need most of all is some more money,' Peter said.

Tony sighed.

'Yes,' he admitted. 'It looks as if we shall have another try at cleaning cars tomorrow. But we still have a few pounds. We can buy some model kits for you to assemble.'

'And we can get a big sheet of hardboard. We can lay it across these trestles and play table tennis,' Julie said.

Tony nodded.

'We'll buy some spare balls from Woolworths while we are in the High Street,' he said. 'They always seem to get trodden on.'

'We can organise all that if you want to make some more nice hutches,' Julie suggested. 'If you tell me the size of the hardboard we can go to the shop and buy it.'

'You won't be able to manage it,' Tony warned. 'Ask them to deliver it in their van.'

Julie laughed and started to mime. She was good at miming.

'Now come along, my good man,' she said, in a posh voice. 'I must have it delivered at once to the Cobweb Club, up the hill.'

They all laughed at her.

'You'll go on the stage one day,' Alan said.

'Well, get me some more nails while you are there,' Tony said. 'We'll stay around here today doing what we can. Tomorrow, the club is closed, except for feeding the animals, of course. It's car washing day, again.'

But it was not to be. Tony's plans were about to be upset, as plans can be quite often.

CHAPTER TEN

THE DARK NIGHT

All went well for the rest of the day and Tony went to bed feeling very pleased. Tomorrow they would earn some more money to buy the things they needed. More children wanted to join. Soon, all the problems would have gone. He wondered if it would be so exciting when things ran smoothly. So much had happened in a short time.

But, most of all, he felt pleased with his older, new found, friends. Abdul, the foreman and, especially, Shan had made him think about deep things, about important things. Already, he realised that life was much more than living to please yourself. There was a big Somebody to please first of all, not in a frightening way, but to please as a friend, your best friend. He wondered if God had been pleased with him today.

When, finally, he went to sleep, he didn't sink into his usual untroubled slumber. Dimly, he thought he heard a noise and, afterwards, remembered thinking that the noise must be from one of the gangs from another estate come to cause trouble and to do as much damage as they could. Soon after, he awoke properly and, unusual for him, was immediately alert.

'Something must be wrong,' he said, half aloud.

He looked around his room in the quarter light. It wasn't pitch black, it never is in the summer, but he guessed, rightly, that it was about the darkest time of the night. He sat up in bed and switched on his light. He jumped out of bed and went to the window. He saw a solitary light across the valley like a pinprick of yellow. Thin clouds scudded across the sky lit by a silver moon until they moved away into the blackness, outside the ring of light. All seemed well. But it wasn't.

He grabbed his clothes and dressed quickly. He opened his door without a sound and slipped into the passage, hoping his parents would be deep in their own sleep and wouldn't hear him. The front door was bolted. Carefully, he tried to slide the bolt so it didn't make any sound. It was difficult. Once, it squeaked loudly. He held his breath and listened, fearful lest his parents came to investigate the sudden noise. But they didn't. He opened the door. The warm night air smelt sweet and clean. He took a deep breath, stepped on to the balcony and closed the door gently behind him. Immediately, he realised what a foolish mistake he had made. He hadn't brought his key! His parents would have to know that he had been on a night prowl. He couldn't get back indoors!

'Stupid!'

He felt angry with himself. All that careful planning and just one mistake. A vital one. He had escaped unnoticed but couldn't return. He wondered what his mother would say. He crept down the concrete stairs and reached the tarmac by the playground. Faintly, his questioning ears picked up another sound, a strange crackling like stiff brown paper being screwed up. The soft wind fanned his face. He turned the corner. Suddenly, he twitched his nostrils and picked up the smell of burning.

'A bonfire?'

He said it in disbelief.

'Not at this time of night!'

A cold thought gripped him and he scooted across the grass, the black grass, to the back of the estate. The moon had gone behind the clouds again. It was difficult to see. He fell over a drain cover and gashed his knee but he hardly noticed the pain. Rounding the final corner, his fears were confirmed. His heart seemed to sink like a heavy stone.

'Fire! Fire! Fire! Fire!'

He paused long enough to grab two metal dustbin lids and, crashing them together, he shouted at the top of his voice.

'Fire! Call the firemen! Fire!'

He threw the lids away and picked up a brick. He ran through the smoke and smashed the window they had repaired. The glass flew in all directions and a splinter struck his cheek. Clouds of smoke billowed through. There wasn't one moment to lose!

He scrambled over the window sill and fell to the concrete floor. His eyes, stung by the smoke, released tears which flowed down his cheeks in rivers. He hoped nobody would think he had been crying, though he felt like it. Boys weren't supposed to cry! He coughed and held his handkerchief to his mouth. The far end of the shed was ablaze and he felt thankful that he hadn't yet hung Abdul's sign over the door. Once, a tin of paint, heated by the flames, shot across the floor and burst against the opposite wall. The gang had struck at a vital part. He guessed they had used paraffin. The flames were yellow and blue.

He groped his way to the hutches and felt blindly for the guinea pigs. He felt a nip on a finger. They were frightened too. He stuffed it down his shirt while he groped for the others. They were all squeaking loudly. At least they were still alive.

'Why doesn't somebody come?'

Nobody was there to help him and he felt nearly exhausted. He didn't realise that he had only been in the shed about a minute. It seemed more like an hour! He staggered over to the window and dropped the animals outside. They would have to take care of themselves. It was the best he could do. The heat was almost unbearable and getting worse. He tried to lift himself over the sill, but he couldn't.

'Help!' he cried, weakly.

His own voice sounded far away. Suddenly, he was aware of somebody with him but he couldn't explain it, for there was nobody there that he could see. Another ball of flame hurtled across the shed, this time in his direction. He shielded his face and turned away, but the tin of paint caught him a glancing blow and he slumped down into the corner into a sea of blackness. The flames licked at his clothing like greedy, hot red tongues. Then the sirens began their wailings. Help was on the way.

Fortunately, the fire station was only down the hill. A resident of The Flats, who hadn't been able to sleep, was making herself a drink in her kitchen and noticed the flames. She telephoned the emergency services immediately.

'It's only an old shed,' the firemen said, when they arrived, but they lost no time in connecting their hoses to the water supply in the pavement. Soon, a steady stream of water was dousing the shed.

The Flats seemed to be alive with people. More turned up every minute. It was Julie who raised the second alarm.

'Where's Tony?' she asked.

Tony's parents heard her.

'He wasn't in his bed,' his mother said. 'He must be here somewhere.'

They looked around quickly.

'Tony!'

'Anybody seen Tony?'

'Tony, where are you?'

Suddenly, something brushed against Julie's leg. She bent down.

'It's one of the guinea pigs!' she exclaimed, gathering it up in her dressing gown.

'The animals couldn't have escaped on their own!'

Tony's father leapt forward.

'He must be in the shed!'

The fire officer pulled him back.

'Leave it to us, sir,' he said. 'It's our job. You must look after your wife. She looks as if she needs you just now.'

'Then be quick, man,' he implored. 'And call an ambulance!'

But the ambulance was already on its way, just in case it was needed.

The firemen leapt through the window into what was left of the shed. It was like entering a cauldron of steam, for the flames had been fierce and a lot of water had been used to quench them.

'Here he is!'

Tony was lying in the corner, face downwards. His

clothes were a soggy black.

'Is he alive?'

The fire officer turned him over gently as a mother would turn over a young baby.

'Just about alive. There must have been a layer of air near the floor.'

They picked Tony up in their arms and handed him through the window.

'Has the ambulance arrived?'

The fire officer was very concerned.

'Yes, sir. It has oxygen on board.'

'Good. Get him away to hospital fast. Take his parents too. Tell them not to stop to dress. Somebody else can bring their clothes later.'

Tony didn't know anything about the ambulance ride to the big hospital, three miles away. He didn't know he had been rescued. He didn't know anything at all. His parents waited outside the examination room while the doctors attended him.

'To think it should all end like this,' Tony's father said, shaking his head in despair. 'If only he had woken us and not tried to rescue the animals on his own. Two of us could have done it. He couldn't do it on his own. The smoke must have been awful.'

'And the heat.'

Tony's mother could only speak in a whisper.

'It must have been like an oven,' she said.

She started to cry again.

Presently a nurse came in.

'I've brought you a cup of tea,' she said. 'No. Please sit down.'

Tony's father had jumped to his feet.

'Is there any news yet?'

'Drink this first,' the nurse said. 'The doctor will be here soon. He will want to tell you himself.'

And they had to be content with that.

Another hour passed. The nurse visited them twice more.

'Doctor will be in to see you soon,' she promised.

Then, suddenly, at last, he came.

'Sit down,' he said.

They had both jumped up.

'You are Tony's parents?'

They nodded, miserably.

'Tell us straight. Will he live?'

Tony's mother wanted to know the whole truth.

'We got him here in time,' the doctor said, smiling. 'It was the water that saved him and the layer of air by the floor.'

'Thank God!'

It was Tony's mother's first spoken prayer for a long time.

'Can we see him?' his father asked.

The doctor was very firm.

'No,' he said. 'Not tonight. He is in intensive care and we have a lot of things to do right now.'

'Tomorrow?'

The doctor smiled again.

'Tomorrow,' he promised. 'No, not tomorrow. To-day! It will soon be light again.'

'May we telephone in the morning?'

'Yes. Please do. Tony may be able to talk to you for a little while when you come. But, don't expect too much for a few days. He has had a very narrow escape and is very ill.'

'How long will he be here?'

The doctor looked thoughtful.

'It's too early to say,' he said. 'Don't expect him home too quickly, though. He's young and will probably make a splendid recovery but it will be a month at least.'

'He's starting a new school in September,' his father said.

The doctor smiled.

'I'm sure he will soon catch up,' he replied. 'He looks a bright lad to me.'

'Thank you for all you have done, doctor.'

Tony's father's eyes were bright with gratitude.

'The porter will order a taxi for you,' the doctor said, brushing aside the thank-yous. 'Try to get some sleep now. You have both had a shock, too. But, don't worry too much. Tony is in very good hands.'

They thanked him again, most warmly, and went down to the night porter's office. The taxi soon came. Dawn was already showing in the east.

'It's not worth going to bed,' Tony's mother said, when they arrived home. 'Besides, I shouldn't sleep.'

But her husband persuaded her to.

'You will be resting,' he said.

They didn't rest for very long.

'Ding. Dong!'

The doorbell rang all through breakfast.

'Just called to see if there was any news.'

'How's Tony?'

'You must be worried stiff.'

'Dreadful, wasn't it?'

A succession of neighbours called to sympathise and to gain information. The Flats were buzzing with excitement.

Later on, there was a gentle knock. Julie and several other members of the club were on the doorstep.

'We've brought some flowers for Tony,' she said. 'Please tell him not to worry about the animals or anything. We just want him to get better so he can come back to us.'

Tony's father took the flowers.

'So do we, Julie,' he said, gently. 'I'll tell him about the animals as soon as I can.'

Julie smiled.

'We'll build a new shed one day,' she said. 'Tell him that!'

A few days passed before Tony could speak to his parents. 'I feel so sore,' he complained, in a whisper. 'They keep changing the dressings on my burns. I wish they wouldn't do it so often.'

'It's all for the best, son,' his father said. 'To make you better so you can come home. They will soon have you on your feet again, you'll see.'

Tony managed a smile.

'I never did like laying in bed, did I?' he said.

His mother smiled back.

'You have to do as you are told here,' she replied. 'Oh, but it is good to see you making progress.'

Each day, their visits grew longer and, soon, Tony was able to sit up in bed. He also started to enjoy his food again. About a fortnight after the fire he asked whether he could have another visitor.

'I have a friend, Mum,' he explained. 'Shan.'

'Yes, I know. She has been to see us three times since the fire. She seems very sensible.'

Tony laughed.

'Sensible is a word you only use when you talk about

children and then not very often,' he said.

'Well, she isn't very old,' his father replied. 'Only half my age, I reckon.'

'Anyway. Do you think she could come in to see me? I want to talk to her.'

Tony's mother nodded.

'I understand,' she said. 'Yes. I am sure she would love to come. It will be nice for you to see somebody else for a change.'

Shan came the next day. She wore the same blue trouser suit that she had worn when she sat on the steps with him. It seemed ages ago.

'I have a more comfortable seat this time,' she laughed, as she pulled a chair close to him.

Tony laughed too.

'It's good of you to come to see me,' he said.

'I was glad to,' Shan replied. 'Fancy you meeting my dad!'

'You didn't tell me he worked for the council.'

'You didn't ask!'

'He was very kind. He's a Christian, too.'

Shan nodded.

'You don't look so bad,' she said, changing the subject. 'Thought you might look a lot worse.'

Tony laughed again.

'That's what I like about you,' he said. 'You are so lavish with your compliments.'

'Lavish!' she repeated. 'Have you been reading a dictionary since you have been in bed?'

Tony sighed.

'I haven't really felt like reading,' he said.

'Shall I read to you?' Shan asked.

'Oh, yes please!'

She opened her handbag and took out a little book.

'These are the Psalms,' she explained. 'They are so beautiful and are especially good to read when you are ill or depressed or in trouble.'

'Then, read it to me, please.'

He sat up as straight as he could.

'It's in a modern translation,' Shan explained. 'It was written, long ago, by David. He became a king and was a direct ancestor of the Lord Jesus who is The King of Kings. Before David was a king he was a shepherd boy. This is one of his songs.'

Because the Lord is my Shepherd, I have everything I need.

He lets me rest in the meadow grass and leads me beside the quiet streams.

He restores my failing health.

He helps me to do what honours Him the most.

Even when walking through the dark valley of death I will not be afraid, for You are close beside me, guarding, guiding all the way.

You provide delicious food for me in the presence of my enemies.

You have welcomed me as Your guest, blessings overflow.

Your goodness and unfailing kindness shall be with me all of my life.

And, afterwards, I will live with You for ever in Your home.

Shan put the little book on the beside cabinet.

'I'll leave it for you to read. It's part of the Bible, of course,' she explained.

They sat in silence for a while. Shan waited, sensing that Tony had something to tell her. Something important.

'Shan.'

'Yes, Tony?'

'Why did you choose that Psalm?'

Shan shrugged her shoulders.

'I don't know,' she said. 'Perhaps God wanted you to hear it.'

Tony smiled.

'God is very real to you, isn't He!'

'Yes. He is. He's my very best Friend.'

'And mine!'

It was Shan's turn to be surprised.

'Yours?'

Tony smiled again.

'When I was in the fire I think I was in the dark valley of death,' he said. 'Somebody was with me and, like David, I wasn't afraid. Somebody has been with me ever since. I knew He was here even when I didn't know other people were by my bed.'

'And who do you think the somebody is?' Shan asked, gently.

'Jesus. God. Your very best Friend.'

Tony's face seemed to light up.

'And He will guard and guide you all the way!'

Shan was radiant.

'Yes. I have asked Him to and He has forgiven me for all the wrong things I have done. It was the first thing I did as soon as I woke up. I wanted to be sure I wasn't just dreaming, you see.'

'Have you told your parents?'

Tony shook his head.

'No,' he said. 'I wanted to tell you first. Now I shall tell Mum and Dad and, when I get home, I'll tell Julie and everybody. And Abdul, of course.

'Good! It helps to tell others,' Shan said. 'May I tell my dad? He will be so pleased!'

'I'd like you to,' Tony said. 'Tell him, there is still a war going on, but now I'm on the right side and I shall listen only to God's voice. Your dad will know what I mean.'

'I think I do too,' Shan said. 'It isn't easy being a Christian. But God is with us and we belong to Him.'

'You'd better go now,' Tony said. 'Otherwise the nurse will tell me off for letting you stay too long.'

Shan laughed.

'Thank you for asking me to come,' she said.

'Will you come again?'

Shan nodded.

'If I can,' she said.

'Thanks. Soon I shall be coming home. Then I'll come up and see you and wash your neighbour's car and ...'

'Shoosh! All in God's good time,' she said, gently. 'All in God's good time.'

CHAPTER ELEVEN

RETURN OF A HERO

Tony's recovery was not as swift as he would have liked.

'But we can't allow you to go home until your burns have healed,' the doctor explained one day. 'You must try to be patient.'

And Tony tried.

Already, the summer holidays were over, his friends were back at school and he was anxious to resume his life and activities. He wanted to see how much the animals had grown, too. Julie, who had visited him twice, with the special permission of the nursing sister in charge, said the animals had grown out of all recognition and she thought one of the females was going to have some babies.

'We have built a temporary shelter for the animals at the back of the estate,' she explained. 'Your dad did most of the work for us. And, we are still cleaning cars and saving money for our new club. I cleaned Abdul's yesterday. All by myself.'

Tony tried hard to be cheerful.

'New club indeed,' he said to her. 'It will take a thousand pounds to buy a shed that size!'

But Julie had just smiled mysteriously.

'You'll be more cheerful when you come home,' she said.

His Christian faith was being severely tested. He didn't like lying in bed! As Shan had said, it wasn't always easy, even when you know you belong to God.

One bright Saturday morning, at about eleven o'clock, his parents arrived wearing their best clothes.

'Hello Mum! Hello Dad! You are a bit early today, aren't you? And looking all poshed up, too!'

Tony's mother laughed.

'We've brought your best suit as well,' she said. 'We've come to take you home!'

'Home!'

Tony nearly leapt out of bed for joy.

'Home! But, the doctor never said ...'

'We all wanted to give you a nice surprise,' his father explained. 'They say you've been a model patient.'

Tony looked doubtful.

'I have complained a bit,' he confessed.

Just then the nurse came in.

'Well, Tony,' she said, cheerfully. 'We shall miss you, but you will prefer to be at home and with your friends. We'll let your dad help you to put your clothes on. You are still sore, aren't you? Never mind. When you are ready come along to the office. Your mum will be waiting for you there.'

'She's quite nice really, dad,' Tony said, after the ladies had left the room. 'Quite nice if you do as she says and drink all the medicine she gives you.'

His father chuckled.

'You won't have to drink any medicine at home,' he said. 'They are very pleased with your progress. Doctor said you'll be at your new school in two or three weeks if you promise to go carefully for a while.

No jumping through windows rescuing animals, though!'

'I promise not to,' Tony replied. 'But I hope this won't be the end of the club. It was just going along nicely when we had the fire. Did they catch the people who set fire to it?'

'No, son. There are too few policemen about to chase every wrongdoer. Besides, I expect they were only boys. Boys in a gang without anything better to do. Pity there aren't a few more do-it-yourself clubs around, I say.'

They went along to the office when they had packed Tony's belongings into a case.

'All ready to go,' the nursing sister in charge said.

'Yes!'

'We shall miss you!'

Tony smiled.

'Thank you for looking after me,' he said. 'I feel a lot better now.'

'Good. We shall be seeing you again, just for a check-up. Now you must be off. The car has just arrived at the main entrance. I'll take you all downstairs.'

'The car?'

Tony thought he would be going home by bus.

'You shouldn't have paid for a car to take us home, dad,' he said, as they made their way through the long corridors of the big hospital.

His parents smiled at him.

'We haven't paid for it,' his mother explained. 'We are all going home in the mayor's car.'

'So that's why we are all poshed up!'

The mayor was at the entrance talking to the matron of the hospital.

'Here comes the very important person,' the matron said, when she saw Tony. 'It isn't every patient of mine who has a ride home with the mayor.'

'I don't understand,' Tony said, shaking his head and wondering how to address the mayor who was a splendid lady in a black dress, fur stole and a glittering gold chain.

'I don't understand at all.'

'You will, Tony,' the mayor said. 'And thank you for your letter. It was very well written. We are all very proud of you and so I have come to take you home. We have another surprise waiting for you when we arrive.'

'I hope you didn't mind me writing to you. And I will pay for the window. I promised.'

The mayor smiled a him and her eyes were moist.

'You have a good son here,' she said to Tony's parents. 'Come. Let's be on our way.'

They all got into the large, black car. There was room to spare. The driver slipped the car into gear and they glided away from the kerb smoothly and quietly.

'I still can't believe I'm not dreaming,' Tony said.

They sped through the streets and soon they were on familiar ground. They passed the fire station, the library and the supermarket. Then they turned up the hill towards The Flats. In the distance, Tony saw a crowd and, as they drew nearer, he heard a cry.

'Here they come!'

Something very special was about to happen.

Looking across the estate Tony could hardly believe his eyes. A crowd of several hundred was waiting for him. For him! Behind the crowd stood a new shed, well, not so much a shed as a building, a splendid new building. Fireproof! Over the door he could clearly see Abdul's sign. 'The Cobweb Club.'

He was completely lost for words. They climbed out of the big car and stood, for a moment, on the pavement. The crowd seemed to stand back for an instant and then, as though an audible signal had been given, they began to walk forward slowly until the children in the crowd could stand it no longer and they broke into a run.

'Welcome back, Tony,' Julie said. 'What do you think of it?'

'It looks marvellous,' he said, finding his voice at last.

'You wait until you see the inside! They haven't finished it on purpose so we can complete the job and have it as we want it. But we helped them put it up.'

Shan was there and her dad. Abdul too. Tony had a special smile for them.

'It all came right in the end,' Shan said.

She looked so happy.

'Yes, Shan. Not only the Cobweb Club. Me as well!'

A clearance was made so the important little group could proceed to the door of the new building. A sudden hush came over them all.

'It gives me the greatest of pleasure to be here ...' the mayor began.

And they all listened to her short speech.

'So, I shall ask the real hero to open the door with this special key,' she concluded. 'Three cheers for Tony and the Cobweb Club!'

Tony grasped the golden key firmly and inserted it

in the lock. It turned easily. Slowly, ever so slowly, he opened the door. He wanted the moment to last a long time and to remember every detail.

'It's like a new beginning,' he said, out loud. 'No cobwebs in this building!'

And Shan smiled to herself, a long, contented smile. For a moment, her eyes met Tony's. A secret communication passed between them.

A new beginning! No cobwebs! That was true of Tony, too!